STRIP FOR MURDER

Mark Bellew presents I Representative, but wha̱̱ ̱̱ ̱̱ ̱really does is supply strippers for private parties. Years ago he made a mistake, and one of his girls was raped, then killed herself. He got out of the business for a while, but realizing that this is the only business he knows, he now keeps a small office just off Wilshire Boulevard. But someone who knows about his past is now sending him threatening letters. The only person Bellew can ask to investigate these letters is Ed Warne, an insurance adjustor who shares the upper floor with him. Warne agrees to do some checking but gets more than he bargains for—because whoever is writing the letters has now committed murder. And who knows how far they'll go to settle this old score.

Also included are two Dolores Hitchens stories from the pages of *Ellery Queen Mystery Magazine*.

"Hitchens work will delight a new audience..."
—Paul Burke, *NB*

Strip for Murder

Plus Two Stories by
Dolores Hitchens

STARK
HOUSE

Stark House Press • Eureka California

STRIP FOR MURDER / IF YOU SEE THIS WOMAN /
BLUEPRINT FOR MURDER

Published by Stark House Press
1315 H Street
Eureka, CA 95501, USA
griffinskye3@sbcglobal.net
www.starkhousepress.com

STRIP FOR MURDER
Originally published by *Mercury Mystery Magazine*, October 1958.

IF YOU SEE THIS WOMAN
Originally published by *Ellery Queen's Mystery Magazine*, January 1966.

BLUEPRINT FOR MURDER
Originally published by *Ellery Queen's Mystery Magazine*, August 1973.

ISBN-13: 978-1-951473-64-8

Book design by Mark Shepard, shepgraphics.com
Cover painting by JT Lindross
Proofreading by Bill Kelly

First Stark House Press Edition: March 2022

Strip for Murder
Dolores Hitchens

CHAPTER ONE

The little man with the graying sideburns, the narrow shoulders and the left-legged limp was a purveyor of female nudity. He kept an office in the Summit Building, just off Wilshire Boulevard, the eighty-five hundred block, and the sign on the door said, *Mark Bellew, Theatrical Representative.*

His office was divided into two rooms. The outer part, the part he had arranged for the inspection of the casual visitor, had walls painted a glacial blue, and there were a couple of couches, blue plastic with copper legs, and some copper-trimmed tables with movie magazines spread out on them. On the walls were some framed big pictures of movie celebrities, and the flattering sentiments inscribed on the photos, as well as the signatures of the stars, had a remarkable resemblance to each other, which was natural since Mr. Bellew had written them all himself.

If you had never seen the inside office you wouldn't have known what Mr. Bellew's real business was, but once in there, there would have been no mistaking it. He had real nudes pasted all over the walls and these were signed by the naked ladies pictured therein. Some had fans resting lightly where they did the most good, and others were simply turned so that a knee provided protection, and some were actually dolled up in something as substantial as a gauze scarf. Fundamentally each was displaying what she looked like in her birthday suit, and Mr. Bellew could tell a prospective customer, without stopping to think about it, just what each lady wanted in cash to appear in public therein.

Mr. Bellew's attitude towards his business was far removed from lechery, and his mild gray eyes had never been known to warm up over an article under discussion, not even an eighteen-year-old redhead with nipples the size of cherries. He kept regular office hours, from nine to six. Twice a week he had a part-time secretary. She was a blonde woman of about twenty-eight who wore horn-rimmed glasses and was studying stenography and bookkeeping three mornings a week. She was a widow with a little girl four years old. In Mr. Bellew's office she was helping support herself as well as getting experience. The correspondence was scant. Most of Bellew's trade was contracted for and paid in person—you might say, in a whisper.

In his personal life Mr. Bellew was even more abstemious than in the office. He never gambled, seldom drank. He lived in an apartment house in Beverly Hills, a very quiet place with a lot of retired well-to-do people in it. He collected oils, sea pictures. He read books on Yoga and mental health and diet. He had not for many a year attended the sort of party for which his beautiful nude ladies were in demand, though occasionally in a nightmare he found himself present. On Sundays he sometimes went fishing on a barge off Santa Monica. His wife was dead, he had no children, and so was quite alone.

On a bright morning in June, Mr. Bellew drove his two-year-old Buick into the proper slot in the parking space behind the building. He got out, locked the car, and entered the building by the rear door. There were two floors. He climbed the stairs, and in passing the door next his own he gave it a quick, sharp, thoughtful glance. It was the office of an insurance adjustor named Edward Warne.

Mr. Bellew unlocked his door and stepped inside, shut the door behind him and glanced around. Then he picked up the mail, which had been dropped through a slot in the door, and went into the inner room. Here he found a light burning in the copper lamp on his desk. He stood for a minute frowning at it, then crossed the room and snapped it off. The Venetian blinds were half-open and the room was filled with morning sunshine.

He sat down and looked quickly through the mail and at sight of one letter in a pale green envelope his mouth tightened and his eyes grew bleak. He put the rest of the mail aside, dropped his hat on it, and sat with the green envelope between his fingers. He was afraid to open it. It would be like the others, and his whole day would be spoiled.

He turned in his chair and poised the letter above the wastebasket, and for a long moment it hung there ready to drop. Mr. Bellew was thinking. He was remembering the day the first green envelope had come, and of how he hadn't taken the message very seriously, had actually thought it might be a very crude joke. .Now he knew there was no joke, and he was scared.

On a sudden afterthought he put the letter on the desk and reached for the lamp, cupped his hand over the brass shade to gauge its heat. The lamp must have been on for many hours. The shade was quite hot.

It was possible, he decided, that the janitress had left the lamp burning after she'd dusted the desk the evening before. Possible but not likely. It was much more probable that the lamp had been switched on by the same hand which had written his name and address on the green envelope.

With an uneasy shrug, as if forcing his mind off his problems, he turned his attention to the rest of the mail. There was a subscription notice from *Variety*, a couple of postcards from girls who were working out of town, a letter from a niece of his in New York, an ad from a theatrical costumer, and a flyer for a jewelry sale.

One of the postcards was from Candy Carroll. She was a big brunette who had been very popular at stag-parties, and was now in Las Vegas doing a strip in one of the gambling club shows. She wrote: *I've worked myself ragged here, Mark, and the heat's getting me. I want to come home. Line up something for me. Love —*

Mark Bellew reached for the phone. When his dialed number answered, he said, "Bellew."

"Well, hello there!" boomed a voice.

"You called yesterday about some talent for your party."

"I sure did, and I want a couple of live ones. You know what I've got in mind."

Mark Bellew's gaze went over to the window where the light was bright. "Yes, I remember." There was nothing in his voice, no disapproval, no censure, no touch of lewdness. "It's rather hard to get a girl who will do what you want," he said carefully. "You understand that, I hope. No reputable dancer would risk it."

"Ah, hell, I don't want those damned high-hat floozies. Get me a live-wire. Get me a good piece of—"

Mr. Bellew broke in hastily. "I have a very attractive girl, tall, black-haired, splendid figure. She's in Las Vegas. She'll come back to L.A. if you make it worth her while and she'll do exactly what you want her to do."

"That's just one, buster."

Mr. Bellew picked up a pencil and tapped it on his desk, watching the tip as if it might break off. "I'll see what I can do about finding another. I might add, though, that Miss Carroll is a most unusual girl. She's easily worth two of the ordinary kind."

"Ha, ha, ha! How about a sample? How about it, huh?"

Mr. Bellew waited, not joining in the laughter. When the laughter was finished they began to discuss the cost of getting Miss Candy Carroll to the party in a professional capacity. Pretty soon when Mr. Bellew began to firm up about the price there were cries of anguish from the other end of the wire. "I'm just the program chairman, goddammit! What d'you think we're running here, Fort Knox?"

"I won't bring her back from Vegas for less than that," Bellew said courteously. "Call me back if you decide you want her."

"Now wait a minute, don't go off half—"

Mr. Bellew hung up the phone.

He sat for some minutes, then got up and walked restlessly around the office. His left knee was stiff, shortening his step on that side. When he was tired or worried the limp was more noticeable. When he was free of care, rested, he was able to control it pretty well.

Finally Bellew opened the inner door, went through the outer office, locked it behind him, rapped on the door to Warne's place.

"Come in," Warne yelled inside.

Warne's office had not been partitioned, but remained a single large room, with walls painted yellow, brown linoleum floor, a desk near the windows, a rank of file-cabinets against the wall.

"Well, well," said Warne from behind the desk. "How's the traffic in flesh today?" He was a big man, in his thirties, with a homely and intelligent face, with clothes that always looked as if he had just gained weight or lost it. He had a scarred eyebrow, the left one, a souvenir of his career as an amateur fighter in college. His tie was crooked. It hadn't been much of a tie to start with; Warne was somewhat color-blind.

Bellew puckered his lips a little. "Your usual tasteless greeting," he reproved Warne. Warne had a stack of forms and letters and an open folder in front of him. "Are you busy?"

"Sit down. Sit down and rest your feet," said Warne, motioning to a chair. He shuffled the papers together and put them into the folder. "I didn't want to work anyhow. I want to look at pictures."

"I didn't bring any pictures," Bellew said. "I came to ask for advice." His gray eyes were watching Warne closely. "You do investigations now and then, don't you, Ed? Sort of detective work, in a way?"

Warne looked surprised. "That's right. I'm also a kind of private eye, but only once in a while and only on insurance business."

"I need some investigating done," Bellew said.

Warne began shaking his head.

"I'm not asking as a favor. For nothing. I'm willing and able to pay for your time." Bellew tapped his breast pocket where his wallet lay. "This is important to me. I'm in a squeeze. It's getting so I dread to come down to the office, dread to begin the day." He licked his lips, still staring at Warne. "I need help. I need professional advice and investigation. I can't go to just anybody, a stranger, a name I pick out of a phone book. I want a friend."

Warne's eyes were a bright blue, direct, searching. "You do seem a little frayed around the edges," he said. "You look as if you'd sprung a spiritual leak. What goes on, anyway?"

"Someone's writing me dirty letters," Bellew said quietly.

Warne's heavy eyebrows went up. "Can you quote?"

Bellew shook his head. "First of all I'd better fill in some of the background," he decided. He seemed suddenly more nervous, less sure of himself. He moved about on the chair, jerked at the crease in his pants' leg, moistened his lips again. "I guess I'll say, to begin with, that I used to be quite a bit different from what I am now.

In the way I thought, and in my moral attitude—" He spread his hands, then clenched them. "I was married. My wife and I were disagreeing most of the time. She didn't like the business I was in. I'd had a legitimate actors' agency, and then I'd gradually begun to specialize on strippers and party girls. I can see now, what she must have figured. Frankly, what she suspected did go on ... now and then."

"I'll bet you were a heller," Warne agreed. Then he added: "How long ago was this?"

"More than twenty years," Bellew answered.

Warne rubbed the side of his nose. "No fire burns forever, huh?"

"Quite right. Remember this, though—I wasn't guilty of the thing that happened to Janie Gordon." His mouth appeared to twist over the name as if at an old, familiar, bitter flavor. "Not the first thing, the thing at the party. Nor the last thing—the final act." He seemed suddenly more stooped, grayer. Warne could see a frost of perspiration on his lips., "Well, to begin at the beginning; about the girl. Janie Gordon came to my office and asked for a party date. She said she was broadminded, wanted to make some quick money. I set her up for a lodge smoker."

Warne was frowning. "What did you know about her?"

"Just what I could see. To me she looked about twenty-two. I believe that was the age she put down on the form. She was slim, medium height. Curly brown hair, cut short. Well developed. Pretty face."

"What happened to her?"

Bellew shook his head. "I'm damned if I know—even at this late date. I attended the smoker. I had five girls, they danced ... well, they skipped around in the altogether and I don't think anyone noticed whether they kept step or not. You know."

Warne nodded.

"As far as I knew, the girls left when the smoker was over. They'd dressed after their dance, come out to drink with the fellows. That's what the program chairman wanted, and that's what they did."

"Except Janie Gordon," Warne surmised dryly.

"No, she was there, dressed, having a drink with some of the lodge members. It was later, when the others had gone—these three boys were supposed to have dragged her into a back room and kept her there the rest of the night." Bellew cleared his throat. "They were rough and drunk. They beat her up. They raped her."

Warne said, "My God, don't you chaperone your girls, get them out of those affairs okay?"

"Since Janie Gordon," Bellew said bitterly, "I've never handled a girl who needed looking after. My girls are veterans. They all know how to handle themselves."

"Well ... go on about this other affair."

"This was told to me later by Mr. Gordon. He said Janie came home—they thought she'd been out dancing with friends—she came home and said she was sick and stayed in bed for almost a week. On the next Sunday, as they were getting ready for church, her parents, I mean, Janie dressed herself up and they thought she was going to church with them. Instead she had them sit down in the living room, and she told them the story of what had happened at the smoker. It had been her first professional engagement. She'd been studying at a little tap-dancing school in Hollywood and needed money for tuition, and had gone to my office on a tip from an acquaintance.

"After she told her parents of the beating and the rape, showed the bruises on her legs and thighs that she'd kept covered by the bedding, she said she was going downtown. Sunday, but that's where she went. She found an office building open and jumped out of the highest window in it."

Warne didn't say anything. He moved an eraser on the desk, dropping it on the folder full of papers and picking it up again.

Bellew said, "I sold my business and gave the money I realized to the Gordons. They were old people—old to be Janie's parents. She was just seventeen by the way. A big girl for her age—they said she always had been."

"How did the Gordons take it?"

"They seemed stunned. I don't think they blamed me,

particularly. I wanted them to go to the police over it and they wouldn't. The cops couldn't bring Janie back. I said the men involved needed a lesson but they were positive the Lord would take care of that end of it. Vengeance is mine.... I guess they were great Bible readers."

"There wasn't any stink," Warne surmised.

"No, no publicity whatever. The girl's suicide was laid to her imaginary difficulties in learning to dance. Some such crap."

Warne thought about it for a couple of minutes. "When did you go back to peddling nudes?"

"In about a year. Hell, I didn't know any trade, the only contacts I had were in this line. I had to make a living. My life at home had straightened out. I'd quit all the helling around and my wife had forgiven me what I'd done before. She trusted me, too. When I set up the new agency she never let out a peep. We were pretty broke by then. I guess she saw I just wanted to make a living."

Warne said, "And what else ... before the letters started coming in?"

"Not a damned thing. Not for more than twenty years."

"Tell me about them."

"I got the first one a couple of months ago. It started out—they all do—with a string of nasty names. For me." He tapped his chest with a finger tip. "Then at the end, the last sentence, there was this: *When it happens again like it did to Janie Gordon, watch out!*" He made a sudden nervous, distracted gesture. "The thing that's gradually chewed into me, got me rattled, is the assurance it *will* happen again! There'll *be* another girl like Janie Gordon, and I'll be blamed and I'll get what I deserve for making it happen to her!" His voice had hoarsened. His hands were trembling. "And I don't see ... I just don't understand how it could happen again. To me. With the girls I have now."

Warne felt an oppressive sense of danger. Bellew was actually on the ragged edge of panic. He hadn't been tying when he said he needed help and advice. He needed both of them, bad.

CHAPTER TWO

"Of course you know what you ought to do," Warne said. "I don't have to spell it out for you, the sensible thing—going to the postoffice agents."

Bellew shook his head after a moment's consideration. "That would involve telling all this story again, all the affair concerning Janie Gordon. I have no intention of going to cops of any kind whatsoever. If you won't help me, I'll look up a private detective."

Warne said, "There may not be much he can do. He won't have the resources of the postoffice agents or the cops."

Bellew's expression became adamant. "I'll have to be satisfied with whatever he can turn up. Since you refuse." His eyes gleamed with a sudden nervous hope.

Warne said uneasily, "I'm not brushing you off. Tell me more about these letters. Are they handwritten? Typed? Where are they mailed? How often? Is there a pattern about their arrival—any day or date, for instance?"

The gleam of hope returned to Bellew's gaze. "They're hand printed. The letter itself, I mean. The envelopes are always typed."

"About the lettering. Do you think it's a man's work or a woman?"

Bellew shrugged, "I don't know. It's even, rounded, rather artistic." He frowned a little, as if thinking his way through the rest of Warne's question. "They're all mailed in downtown L. A. I hadn't noticed a pattern, any particular interval between, or any certain day."

Warne had picked up the pen and was writing on a sheet of paper. He tossed the written tab across the desk towards Bellew. "Here's the name and business address of an expert on documents. Take the letters to him. He can tell you the kind of paper, the make and age of typewriter, and can probably give you a lot of details about the person doing the lettering. It's amazing what these boys can get off a sheet of paper."

Bellew took the tab of paper with a hint of reluctance. "I had thought about fingerprints."

Warne nodded. "Okay, then, bring them here first and I'll test them for you."

"I've been burning them," Bellew admitted. "The only one I have now is the one that came this morning."

Warne had risen from his chair. "Well, bring that."

Bellew stuck the scratch tab into his pocket and hurried out, came back in a minute or so with the green envelope held gingerly by one corner between his thumb and forefinger. He put it down in front of Warne as though it had the explosive possibilities of a bomb. He said with a touch of strain in his tone, "I told you, didn't I, that the things begin with a lot of—of obscenities. About me. The person who wrote those letters to me has a twisted mind," Bellew declared. "That's the most obvious thing about him. Or her."

"You'd better have more than that," Warne said grimly. He had carefully slit the green envelope, and now withdrew a sheet of matching shade and quality. Using the letter-opener as a lever, he lifted the top of the folded sheet, spread it flat. For a moment both he and Bellew stood in an attitude of transfixed astonishment, Bellew's even more indicative of shock, and staring at the completely blank page.

"Since when?" Warne asked quietly after a moment.

Bellew looked positively ill with emotional impact. He rubbed his face with his hand, distorting his features. He looked at Warne as if absolutely stunned. "It's fiendish," he whispered.

"Well, prints are what we have here—if anything," Warne said philosophically. He started to move, but Bellew reached across the desk and grabbed his wrist.

"Why?" he cried hoarsely. "Why the change from obscenities and the promise of trouble to come? Why ... nothing?"

"I think we've got a psychologist on our hands," Warne answered. He disengaged Bellew's grip, went across the office to a file cabinet and took out a small black box containing a fingerprint kit. He brought it back to the desk, sat down to open it. Bellew again sank into his own chair. "He's figured that you've absorbed the intended message. He doesn't have to risk writing it out." Warne threw a sharp glance at Bellew. "He knows you pretty well, I'd say."

Warne had opened a small black vial, taken up a delicate camelhair brush, and was dusting the pale green sheet for signs of prints. Almost at once several appeared. The tiny black whorls seemed to spring up on the paper.

"I'll be damned," Warne said in puzzlement.

"What is it? What does it mean?"

"A kid." Warne nodded at the page. "See how small they are?"

"Why, a kid couldn't write such letters!" Bellew cried.

"You're right, this kid is almost too young to write anything. But the kid had its mits on this sheet of paper. Or else the prints were planted to confuse you." Warne tossed the paper aside and bent a steely glance on the other man, "Who knows you, Bellew, who also knew you when Janie Gordon killed herself? Who lives close enough and intimately enough to keep an eye on you, to sense your moods, to get their kicks out of your fright and despair?"

"Nobody ... nobody ... nobody—" Bellew was almost crying. He seemed like a man possessed. "The only people who knew the truth about Janie Gordon's suicide were her parents, and me."

"How can you be sure?" Warne demanded. "How do you know they didn't tell other people, people you yourself were acquainted with?"

Bellew leaned across the desk. "They told me." He pounded his flat palms on the mahogany. "They promised me, swore to me— no one but the three of us would know what had happened to their girl. And in return they made me swear that I'd never tell anybody." His face twisted. "Now I've broken that promise. I've told you."

"It's no secret," Warne said dryly, "if those letters have been what you say they are. Beside that, what about your wife? Didn't she know the story?"

Bellew's face worked for a moment and then he burst forth with,

"Yes, I did tell my wife. I confessed what had happened and why I felt I had to make amends, not just by paying the money to the girl's parents but by getting out of the business as well."

"And then your wife—"

"She wouldn't have told a soul," Bellew insisted. "What Sarah knew died when she died, lies in the grave with her."

"All right. We'll leave it that way, then. Your wife never told anyone else the story of Janie Gordon's suicide." His eyes were cold on Bellew's nervous face. "But somehow, someone found out. Whoever it is hates you, Bellew. That hatred has in it the desire to torment. I don't see any other purpose behind this thing. According to what you've told me, there's not a warning intended, kindly or otherwise. It's a prophesy. Is that right?"

"Yes, that's it. It's going to happen again. I'll get what's coming to me, then."

"But on the other hand, you figure you must be safe because of the care you've taken, choosing your girls."

Bellew said, "I guess I ought to get out of the business."

"That might be the answer," Warne agreed. "You're nearing the age when most people retire, anyway. Or, if you can afford a vacation, this would be a good time to take it."

Bellew nodded miserably, as if the idea were familiar. "I could just close the office and stay home. The trouble is, I haven't a lot of money laid by."

"Give yourself another week," Warne said finally. "I'll have a little free time by then. Maybe another letter will come, something in it we can work with. Meanwhile take this blank page and the envelope to the man I told you about, and find out what he can tell you."

Bellew looked so wretched that Warne added, "It'll be a start."

"All right." Bellew went back to his own office and put the green envelope on his desk, sat down with a sigh. His dulled eyes were filled with misery. After a moment he folded his hands, one over the other, and laid his head down on them. He made a picture of complete defeat.

The phone rang. Bellew lifted his head. For a moment he

seemed undecided about answering. Then he lifted the phone and said, "Bellew."

"Say, doggone it, you run a funny damned kind of a business. Here I'm trying to make a deal, and you cut me off and I can't get you for over a half-hour."

"I stepped out," Bellew said flatly.

"Well, about this girl in Las Vegas. I talked it over with the Finance Chairman—he holds the dough—and after some argument he okayed the price you quoted. I told him what you said about her and he thinks she might fill the bill. We'll spread the word she's something special. Now, she'll be the main attraction, but we want you to line us up two or three more women. Nothing expensive. We want someone who'll put on a little show and won't mind having a little fun afterwards."

"Yes, I understand." Bellew sounded utterly weary and indifferent. The other man seemed to sense the change in him. "You won't have any trouble getting what we want, will you?"

"No, not at all."

"Okay, then. I'll pass the word. Don't forget the date."

"I wrote the date down," Bellew said.

When he hung up the phone, he lifted it at once, called the telegraph office and dictated a wire to Candy Carroll. He specified the date and the price. Candy would know by the sum mentioned what was expected of her, more or less. She was not only beautiful, with a superb figure and a strikingly attractive face, but she was shrewd and business-like and completely capable of looking after herself. He needn't have any worries about Candy, how she would perform or how she would be treated.

He had to pick out three other girls, though. The party promised to be wet, rowdy and capricious. He had to choose carefully from his available entertainers. Bellew opened a drawer of his desk and dipped out a handful of cards. Each had a picture glued to its left-hand corner, and the girl's name, measurements and specialties if any, filled the rest of the card.

There was a nervous frown between Bellew's brows as he checked through the cards, discarding most of them but finally laying a half-dozen aside. He picked up the phone again, began dialing the numbers listed.

Gradually the look of tension and depression faded from his face. He was concentrating on the job at hand, and the letters were almost forgotten.

Candy Carroll took a cab from the Greyhound Bus direct to Bellew's office. It was the second morning after his interview with Warne. Candy walked in, shoulders back to display her amazing bosom. Bellew's part time secretary was in the office, the outer room, seated at a desk with a typewriter. The mousy blonde in the horn-rimmed glasses made a striking foil for the big gorgeous brunette.

Candy paused by Mrs. Shafer's desk, lit a cigarette before speaking. "Will you tell Mr. Bellew I'm here? I'm Miss Carroll."

Mrs. Shafer rose quickly. "Just a moment, please." She went to the door of the inner room and rapped. "Mr. Bellew?"

"Come in," said Bellew's voice.

She opened the door a mere crack and said primly, "A Miss Carroll is here."

Bellew appeared in the doorway in another moment. He smiled at Candy. "Come inside." As she walked towards him he studied her critically, as he might have examined a high-stepping filly he was about to enter in a race. A faint, approving smile touched his lips. She went past him, swinging her hips. She was several inches taller than Bellew.

In the inner office she sat down, stretched her graceful legs, crossed her ankles and flipped ashes into the tray on Bellew's desk. "Thank God you got me out of Vegas," she said in a husky tone. "That place is a frying pan in the summer."

Bellew sat down behind his desk. He folded his hands on the blotter. "This Lodge date will pay your rent and feed you for a while. Meanwhile I'll try to line up something more permanent. The supper clubs are using a lot of strip acts now. I'll try to get you something good." He hesitated, and then with his gaze on Candy's figure he said, "You've put on a little weight, haven't you?"

She patted her midsection. "I'll take it off right away."

"I don't know. It rather becomes you," Bellew said thoughtfully.

"My clothes are all too tight." She plucked at the pink jersey.

"No, not really."

She looked at him narrowly through thick black lashes. For a moment, behind a spurt of cigarette smoke, her expression was a mixture of surprise and wry amusement; and then she must have noticed his strictly cool and commercial attitude. She straightened her face quickly. She thought, he hasn't changed a bit. He's the same cold fish. "Tell me about the date."

Bellew picked up a written memorandum. "They call themselves the Business Men's All-America Patriots. I think they started out, about ten years ago, as a sort of anti-Communist thing, a bunch of merchants and bankers eager to root out disloyalty. Well, the noble sentiments seem to have gone down the drain. The brothers discovered how much fun they could have and probably how trusting their wives were, while they were supposed to be searching for Reds. They're strictly for kicks."

"Oh, I've met boys like that before," Candy said off-handedly, "They're like little kids. They yap a lot of high and mighty stuff about keeping the country clean, and then their pockets are full of dirty pictures. They pinch the butt off any woman who makes the mistake of stopping near them. And they'll wave a flag in her face while they're doing it." Candy giggled.

Her air of light-hearted, knowing sophistication was soothing to Bellew. Candy knew what the score was. If you were worried about what had been written in a lot of anonymous letters, if you were nervous almost to the point of sickness over an imaginary and impending disaster, Candy was just the article you needed. She knew how to look after herself. In her air of competence, in the strength of her long firm legs and shapely torso, was just the reassurance Bellew needed.

CHAPTER THREE

Warne came into Bellew's outer office just as Candy Carroll was leaving. The big brunette gave him a lazy stare with a touch of interest in it, and Warne found himself wondering what sort of woman actually inhabited the luscious, full-blown body. Bellew greeted him at the inner door, led the way back to the desk. Bellew seemed cheerful and lively today.

Warne sat down and said, "What did you hear from the document expert?"

Bellew rustled some papers, his gaze growing thoughtful. "Oh, quite a bit. All interesting. The page is Beaton's Copperhill Bond, an expensive grade of social writing paper. Sold all over the country, though, so it doesn't lead anywhere particularly. The envelope, though it looks the same, isn't. It's a much cheaper grade of stock. Isn't manufactured any more, either. The company which made it, several years ago, tried to promote a line of tinted business paper. But it didn't catch on."

"That's damned interesting," Warne said.

"The document expert advanced the idea that the person writing the letter might have access to a store of these old envelopes, and is using them up."

"What about the typing?"

"It was done on a new machine, fresh ribbon. An Underwood. There are slight irregularities even in new type—I guess in your business you're familiar with all this. Anyway, the expert can identify the machine if we ever locate it. And he can eliminate the others."

"Well, that's elementary for those fellows."

"He said that the typist is pretty good. Not a professional, perhaps, but close to it." Bellew cleared his throat. "He thinks it's a woman."

Warne said, "Do any candidates come to mind?"

"No. Not one. I wish, though—" Bellew stretched in his chair, the first sign of a need to relieve an inner strain. "I wish you'd look up these people, Janie's parents, and talk to them. Perhaps not just … just openly about their daughter. Maybe you could pretend to be investigating some insurance claim or other, the sort of thing you ordinarily do, ask them about some imaginary character as a chance to meet them."

"What do you want to know?" Warne asked with a trace of sharpness.

"Their general condition. Financial and otherwise. Whether they've remained normal and friendly people, haven't turned secretive or embittered."

"Do you have any idea where they might be living after all these years?"

Bellew put his hands on the desk, palms flat. "There's a Josiah Gray Gordon listed in the telephone book. Lives on the beach above Santa Monica, according to the address. Of course it doesn't have to be the same man. But that was the name of Janie Gordon's father."

"You've got a good memory."

"It's engraved here," Bellew said seriously, tapping his forehead.

"I'll tell you what I'll do," Warne said. "I have an errand out that way, Redondo Beach, and if I finish in time this afternoon I'll chase up the coast and see what Josiah Gray Gordon looks like." Bellew took out his wallet and began to extract a twenty dollar bill, and Warne added, "Don't be in such a rush to give your money away."

"I should pay for your gas, anyway," Bellew said.

"I'll let you know when I'm out of gas."

"Well … tell you what, how about my treating for dinner tonight?"

Warne said, "I'm not like you. I've got a date." He jerked his head in a sarcastic nod, got up and walked out. In the outer office he hesitated, thinking. Hell, Bellew would be better off with a private detective, one who could give the thing his full attention.

Mrs. Shafer pushed up her glasses and peered at him through the lenses. "Is there something you forgot?" she wondered.

"No, I guess not."

Warne had always thought her pretty plain behind those horn rims, but now he caught a hint of softness and warmth. The white blouse was neat and business-like, no ruffles, no deep-V neck, no tightness across the breasts.

Warne leaned on the desk. "It just occurred to me to wonder why in the devil you want to work here."

Her eyes widened behind the glasses. "Why, Mr. Bellew's a fine man to work for. I couldn't ask for a nicer employer."

"I was thinking of his line of business."

If he thought he might rouse any primness or confusion, he was wrong. She kept a direct look on his face. "Mr. Bellew supplies a commodity which is in demand. Isn't that the function of a business, any business?"

"You surprise me," Warne said frankly.

She smiled a little. She removed the glasses, folded them on the desk, rested the backs of her hands briefly on her eyes as if to relax them. Without the horn rims, Warne thought, she looked much younger and less serious. She could pass for twenty-five. She had fair skin, and the ash-blonde hair flattered it, brought out the faint color. "I'm not the prude you thought me." He started to protest, but she waved it off. "You've been in and out for months, friendly with Mr. Bellew—and every glance you've ever paid me asked why on earth Bellew should keep such an old maid in the office." She laughed lightly. "Especially with all those well-upholstered dolls parading into the place."

"I've figured out one thing," Warne said boldly. "You wear the specs and the business garb so he won't draft you for a strip spot."

"I dress the way I like." She got up, went over to a file cabinet, then turned to glance back at Warne. He wondered if she'd maneuvered so that he would notice her legs. They were graceful and shapely, inside sheer nylon hose. Her black skirt fitted snugly over slim hips.

Warne said, "How about dinner, so I can quiz you some more?"

She picked a card from the cabinet, studied it. "I'm sorry. I have a little girl to feed."

"Bring the kid along. I like 'em."

She threw him a quick look. "No, I meant I'd have to go home first, fix her dinner and get her into bed, call a sitter, before I could think about a date."

"And what would you think, then? Yes, or no?"

He couldn't read her eyes. Was she amused? Interested? Finally she said, "How about eight? Is that too late for your dinner?"

"I love dinner at eight. It's so fashionable."

She gave him her address and phone number, and he jotted them down. When he got back to his own office, the phone was ringing. He lifted the receiver and found Bellew on the wire.

"I heard that!" Bellew said. "What was this business about your already having a date?"

"'My God, you didn't think I'd want to go out with you!" Warne answered, and hung up.

At a quarter of three, in a cove on the coast above Santa Monica, Warne pulled to the side of the highway to size up the spot. It was a collection of a dozen-odd homes, big ones. A wall topped by greenery shut off most of the view from the highway, but he could see that all of the houses were somewhat alike, ranch style, tile roofs and burned adobe brick. Further down the highway, he could see a big arched entry. He drove towards it.

Iron gates stood ajar. The eucalyptus threw shadows over everything, the sloping street, the dark green lawns, the low houses. Warne drove through the gateway, turned right, circled around looking at numbers on the houses.

He was surprised, somewhat uneasy. This wasn't the kind of place he would have expected to find the parents of Janie Gordon. Though Bellew hadn't exactly said so, he had gotten the impression that they were poor as well as old. Bellew had turned over to them, as penance money, what he had realized from the sale of his agency. The kind of business he had, the agency couldn't have brought more than a few thousand. Most of the trade existed in Bellew's hat.

But these houses, set in the vast green lawns, smelled of money.

Big money. No one lived here without laying out at least fifty thousand for a home. Perhaps more.

Warne drove around, and made up his mind that Bellew had sent him on a wild goose chase. This wasn't the right Gordon, couldn't be.

He found the house. A long porch spread across the front of it. On the tile floor of the porch were heaps of gay cushions, low tables, chrome-and-canvas lounges.

Warne parked the car and got out. He went up the bricked walk to the porch, to the door, and pressed a button on the wall.

The door opened in a couple of minutes. The man who looked out at him was tall, lean, and tanned. About twenty-two or twenty-three, Warne thought. Muscular, the whipcord kind. His hair was almost white, or sun-bleached that way, butch cut. His eyes seemed unnaturally blue. He wore a bright orange shirt, unbuttoned, tucked at the waist into tight white pants, the kind the native boys were supposed to prefer in the Caribbean. "Yes, sir?" he said in a quiet, deep voice.

"My name is Warne. I'm an insurance adjustor." Warne took out a card and offered it, but the young man didn't appear to want it. He just glanced at it and nodded. "I'm trying to locate a Mr. Gordon. Josiah Gray Gordon. Does he live here?"

"Yes, he does." The look was direct, perhaps a little belligerent. "Do you have an appointment?" When Warne shook his head, the young man added, "Mr. Gordon is quite elderly. He's been ill. He doesn't see anyone unless it's very important."

"This is very important."

"You'll have to explain your business, what you want to know, to me. I screen all of Mr. Gordon's visitors."

Warne decided to try a little bluff. "This is a police matter, in a way," he said guardedly. "We're trying to handle it as quietly as possible. The insurance people are discreet—you know that, of course." The man in the doorway nodded automatically, so Warne went on. "This claim is being settled with almost a minimum of investigation. Actually, we're cutting corners where I suppose we shouldn't. You understand?"

The man with the young lean face nodded after a moment. "I see. And what does Mr. Gordon—an old man, almost helpless—have to do with your little mystery?" The tone was clipped.

Jesus, he's suspicious, Warne thought. "I don't know," he said with pretended frankness. "It's merely a matter of identification. He might help us. Or perhaps not."

The other man seemed to be having trouble pinning Warne down. "Just what sort of help would you require? A court appearance?" Warne was shaking his head. The younger man continued, "His eyes aren't what they used to be. If you want him to look at pictures—"

"I wish to describe a certain person to Mr. Gordon. Then, without any help or further reminder, I want to see whether he can name that person."

The man in the Caribbean pants seemed to breathe easier. "Well, write out this description, this person you're investigating, and I'll read it to Mr. Gordon and report back."

"I wish it could be handled that way," Warne said, as if the young man had really wanted to help. "It's too confidential a matter. It's too close—much too close—to what the police would consider their territory."

He had the young man's curiosity up; that was obvious. But there was still wariness, hesitation. And all at once Warne didn't give a damn.

He shrugged his shoulders. "Oh, hell. Skip it, will you?"

"Wait a minute. Might I see your identification again?"

Warne took out the card, re-offered it. The young man took it but said, "Don't you have more than this? Something put out by your company, for example, with your picture on it?"

Warne displayed the ID in his wallet, and the other nodded. Warne meanwhile tried to figure it out. There had been a change, all right. He was going to get inside. But why? He had a hunch that the whispery hint of cops might have done the trick. Butch Cut wanted to listen, had no intention now of letting Warne get away. Well, it was interesting, but he'd bet his shirt this Mr. Gordon still wasn't his cookie.

The man in the doorway was stepping aside, showing the way into a shadowy tile-floored hall; but the bright blue eyes were cold as glacial ice. "Mr. Gordon is in the solarium."

He padded away on his straw beach sandals. Warne followed. They went past some closed doors, an arch that opened to a patio, and then at the back of the house there was a roofless room, glassed-in, full of tropical greenery. On a small paved area at the center was a big canvas umbrella and under it sat a fragile old man in a modern collapsible wheel-chair. He was all wrapped up in blankets. He didn't look hot, though. He looked like a crushed copper shell of a man, drained of blood and life, set here to toast in the heat of the roofless room. Only his eyes moved as they came closer.

A hearing-aid was clamped to a dried copper ear. The younger man spoke into it. "Uncle Gray, there's someone to see you. Wants to ask a question. It's about an insurance claim. Not yours, someone else's."

Warne said, "He's putting in a claim?"

"There's no question, in his case. You know that above a certain age, when a man lives so long, life insurance is to be paid as if the insured had died."

"He's that old?" Warne asked with interest.

"He's that old."

A thin cackle of sound dribbled from the old man's lips. "I beat 'em, I beat 'em all."

The young man brought up two white iron chairs, placed them close to the old man, sat down in one. Warne got it now. His errand was going to be weighed and judged, not by old Mr. Gordon, but by the watch-dog.

Warne spoke directly to Gordon. "We are trying to check the identity of a person putting in a claim for injuries. He's given various references, but the others haven't been definite enough. We have to be sure that this person is the person insured many years ago. You understand, time makes changes."

"You bet it does," said the cracked voice.

Warne pretended to hesitate. "I understood that your wife

might help us, also. Could we have her here?"

"Not unless you want to dig her up," came the surprisingly sharp retort. "She's been dead nearly twenty years."

"I see." Warne filed it away. He'd check death notices later. From the impatient attitude of the young man, he judged that he had better make this interview brisk, short and innocent. "I'll run over the description of this person, and you let me know if you can identify him, give him a name." Quickly, picking details from his memory, he rattled off item after item. When he was through the bald brown head was shaking.

"Never heard of such a feller," said Josiah Gray Gordon.

The young man stood up quickly, touched the back of Warne's' chair. Warne rose to go. "Thank you very much," he said to the old man.

"Welcome."

As soon as he was gone there would be some thinking done, some talking, too. The old man and Native Boy would have things to chew over, or he missed his guess. But Warne, too, had things to think about.

The description he had rattled off had been Bellew's. And by subtle changes in the copper face he knew that Mr. Josiah Gray Gordon had recognized it.

Janie Gordon's papa had come a long, long way.

CHAPTER FOUR

Warne didn't go back to the office. It was after five when he got back into L.A.; he went directly to his apartment in North Hollywood. He changed his clothes, bathing and shaving in the process, and then sat down with the paper in his living room. After a while he mixed himself a drink, rye whiskey and water, and took it back to his chair. The apartment was darkening. He reached for the lamp, switched it on. It was then that the telephone rang.

He picked up the receiver. "Warne speaking."

A smooth, light feminine voice said into his ear, "Mr. Warne, I'd like to pass on a word of caution. You're meddling in things which don't concern you. Unhealthy things."

Warne asked, "Are you Bellew's letter writer?"

There was momentary silence, as if he had said the wrong thing, the unexpected thing. Then: "I'm trying to do you a favor."

"Oh, undoubtedly. What are you setting Bellew up for? A shakedown? There are fatter sheep in these Hollywoods. He's hardly worth the bother."

A touch of impatience marred the smooth tone. "For your information, I have never had contact with a person named Bellew."

"Then you should stop writing him those nasty letters."

An angry exclamation reached him over the wire. "You are deliberately pretending not to understand. Or you hope you'll confuse me. I don't confuse easily, Mr. Warne. For the last time, I'll repeat my message. Don't meddle in this old affair. Like dynamite, age has made it dangerous. And most dangerous for you."

"*Boom!*" Warne yelled into the phone. There was a gasp of rage and the line went dead. Warne went back to his paper.

The phone rang again in a moment. Warne took up the receiver and said carefully, "This is the deputy coroner. Mr. Warne has just shot himself in the head." He expected some reaction, but there was nothing, just dead silence; so finally Warne said, "Hello," in his normal voice.

Bellew cried, "My God, you almost scared me senseless! What was all that crap about shooting yourself?"

"Just a gag."

"Did you go see Gordon?"

"Yes, I saw him. He's about ninety years old. Lives in a beautiful big home in a private subdivision. Big trees, private beach, wall all around the place. Has a young man who acts as a personal bodyguard and trouble-shooter. Plus other help I didn't get to see."

"Warne, I can't understand you. Obviously this isn't the same man, Janie Gordon's father. Why, the mere idea is fantastic!"

"Is it? Tell me why?"

"Gordon and his wife were the plainest kind of people. She wore a cotton housedress all the time, even in my office, even at the funeral. She hadn't any gloves and I could see how work-worn her hands were, big knobby knuckles and broken nails."

"Look, Bellew, this is your man. Make no mistake about that."

"It can't be."

"He's acquired a hell of a lot of money somehow. Maybe what you gave him, gave him a start. How much was it?"

"A few thousand. He was going to buy a ticket back to the farm."

"Well, he detoured considerably. He's living the life of a millionaire, or anyway a half-millionaire, and he's got more money coming from an insurance company because he's outlived the mortality tables. Now, does the age conform with the man you want?"

"Yes, he'd be very old now. But this man can't be Janie Gordon's father." Bellew was determined to reject Warne's opinion.

"Maybe he bought a piece of land somewhere and it turned out to have oil on it. Or uranium."

"I don't like fairy tales," Bellew snapped.

"He's living one," Warne pointed out. "But the question is easily settled. Go take a look at him."

"Well ..." Bellew seemed at a loss now. "Well, suppose it is the

Gordon I knew? Suppose he has in some mysterious way become rich? It doesn't outline a course of action."

"As I see it, you had two possible ideas in mind. You wanted to know if Gordon or his wife could have become deranged, senile perhaps, and have let their daughter's death become an obsession. Or, on the other hand, if they might be down on their luck and softening you up for blackmail?" He waited; Bellew muttered an agreement. "You've answered the questions, then. Mr. Gordon has all his wits about him, he's cool and sharp as a tack. He has money, and besides that he's all set to put the bite on an insurance outfit. My guess—it's a hefty bite. I don't think he's working over a hot typewriter on those letters you're getting, or has a secretary doing it, either."

"Yes, that's out of the way." Bellew waited a moment, then asked, "Are you getting ready to take Mrs. Shafer to dinner?"

"I'm ready now. I'm just killing time. Incidentally, just before you called I heard from somebody else." He repeated for Bellew's benefit the short conversation with the unknown woman. "The important thing about this call isn't the warning, which was stupid. It's the speed with which someone found out I was working for you."

Bellew's words tumbled over each other in agitation. "I told you this letter writer was reading my mind! It's uncanny! Here I did no more than talk briefly to you a couple of days ago, and all you did was to check on one party—and already the word's out."

"This woman has a pipeline into your place somehow. What about dancers, strip girls you've placed lately or Mrs. Shafer?"

"You think I'd talk to them about *this*?"

"No. No, I guess you wouldn't."

There was a short space of waiting and then Bellew said, as if completely disheartened, "I'll see you tomorrow."

"Maybe you'll have another letter by then."

"Oh, God!"

Sandra Shafer lived in a neat bungalow in West L.A. It wasn't exactly new, but it was roomy and well-tended. Warne rang the bell at two minutes of eight, and she opened the door immediately. She had her hair curled softly now, shoulder length instead of tucked back of her ears. She wore a blue satin dress, short but dressy, with an off-shoulder bodice that showed a lot of fine creamy skin. She said, "Come inside while I grab a wrap. I want you to meet my aunt. She volunteered to stay with Dotty tonight."

An elderly woman sat on a couch across the room. She wore a severe black dress without even a touch of white at the neck. To Warne her face had a stringy hardness, the eyes seemed beady and intent. She looked Warne over as if his dishonorable intentions were visible.

"How do you do?" Warne said politely.

"Fine. Are you from the office where Sandra works part time?"

"I'm an insurance adjustor," Warne said. "I have an office next Bellew's."

"What do you do?"

Warne said, "I handle investigations and adjustments for claims filed against some of the smaller insurance companies—firms which don't keep a regional office here, or don't keep a full staff."

She thought it over, lips pressed together. "You help the insurance companies rob people of what's coming to them," she decided, as if translating what he had told her. Sandra Shafer said, "Oh, Aunt Faye!"

"If that was my job, I'd quit it," Warne said.

She sniffed and turned her attention to his clothes. "Well, you seem to be doing well at it."

"It's a living." Warne felt as if he were on trial, and he reacted with anger until he forced himself past the ill-humor, and assumed the tolerance which was his usual attitude. Warne winked at the younger woman. "I'm fresh out of homeless orphans and widows at the moment, however."

"Even so," Aunt Faye sneered, "it's an improvement over that other man's kind of work, that Mr. Bellew."

Warne picked up his ears. "You disapprove of Mr. Bellew?"

"Some day before too long, Sandra will be raped in that office," Aunt Faye said. "I feel it in my bones."

With a gasp of exasperation, Sandra Shafer led the way outdoors. She had a white wool stole over her arm, a small gilt purse in her hand. On the walk, she looked at him cautiously. "She's terribly narrow and opinionated, I know. I'm apologizing for her, for what she said."

"Forget it," Warne said. "Lots of little old women fall into a pattern of chronic disapproval and alarm, and can't seem to crawl out. Where do we eat?"

"Do you really want me to suggest something, or do you have a favorite hangout you'd prefer?" she asked, with the directness he liked.

"Well, to be frank I'd like a steak, a big one."

"How about the Smoke House?"

"That's dandy."

After the dinner they took in a show in Hollywood, and then they had a couple of drinks in a bar which kept a gypsy violinist. Over the drinks Sandra explained that tomorrow, following early classes, she worked in a building-and-loan office. When she had finished the bookkeeping course they wanted her permanently, full time, and she supposed that this would be the end of her job with Bellew. "It's actually not as interesting as working there next to you," she said. "There's a certain fascination about theatrical people, even if represented by an over-bosomed stripper. A certain life and change—I guess you could say, uncertainty."

"Bellew's certainly been in it a long time," Warne said icily.

She sipped at her tall green drink. "I don't think he's happy at it, though."

"Don't you? Why not?"

"Lately he's been worried and absent-minded. I wonder if he's making enough to support himself and keep the office going."

"If you handle his bookkeeping, you should know."

She smiled at him. "I am beginning to believe that any bookkeeping done, is done in Mr. Bellew's head. I write letters and keep track of the rent and utilities for the office. I keep the files up to date, the girls' addresses, new phone numbers, other changes. Mostly I think I'm a kind of window-dressing."

At a quarter past one, at her door, Sandra offered him her lips in goodbye. The kiss was warm, sincere, inviting. With half his thoughts Warne told himself: she's been there, next door in Bellew's office, all these months—and I never wasted a glance at her! With the other half he was busy thinking up an excuse for another date. This one had been a spur of the moment affair. Maybe she liked them that way.

"See you next week," she whispered.

"Not sooner?"

"I don't go out much."

"If it's a matter of paying a sitter—"

"No, usually I get Aunt Faye and she comes for nothing. I wouldn't feel right, gadding a lot, with Dotty at home."

"Next week, then."

"Goodnight."

She let him kiss her again.

He crossed Bellew's outer office, which was empty, and rapped at the inner door, and Bellew's voice said, "Come on in."

"You caught me just as I was going out."

Bellew seemed pale, and there were pouches under his eyes. "You're busy today?"

"As usual." Warne had a leather folder in his hands, zippered shut. In it were the details of the malpractice suit filed against a doctor covered by one of the insurance companies Warne worked for.

"I've had another idea," Bellew said. "I want you to check up on the men involved in the Janie Gordon case. The creeps who attacked her."

"Now we're getting into delicate territory," Warne said. "No charge was ever made against them. They're in the clear like birds. They won't love me for coming around bearing old tales."

"It won't hurt to check," Bellew said stubbornly.

Warne could see that something was disturbing the older man. "You got another letter?" Warne asked.

Bellew shook his head. "I have a horrible feeling—since seeing that blank page—that there won't be any more."

"That should make you feel better," Warne said, staring at him closely.

"I think the ... the time of prophecy is at hand. That's what the blank page means." Bellew's throat was working as if he were trying to swallow a strangling lump. "It's going to happen again."

"My God, they've really got you going."

Bellew stood up behind the desk. He started to move away, and then seemed to forget the errand he was about to do; he stood there, shrunken, and when his hands scratched about on the blotter, Warne could see his fingers shake. "You see, there's a party coming up. The sort of thing ... exactly the sort of thing that Janie Gordon went to. Tomorrow night. I've lined up Candy Carroll and three other girls. They're all veterans, they all know the ropes. I'd swear that any one of them could handle a dozen gorillas—if the gorillas were getting fresh."

"Then what are you worried about?"

"I don't know." Bellew rubbed a hand down over his face. His eyes were sick, washed-out. "I've got a crazy notion those same men might be there. By some freak of chance. That's why I wanted you to look them up."

"You have their names and addresses?" Warne asked incredulously.

"No."

"How would I find them, then?"

"Go back to Josiah Gordon. His daughter told him who those men were."

It occurred to Warne that the strain caused by the threatening letters had actually unhinged Bellew's mind.

CHAPTER FIVE

Though Warne had a great deal to do that morning and could scarcely spare the time, he sat down and forced himself to appear calm. Across the desk, Bellew in turn fell into his chair, still shaky and upset. Warne said, "It's been more than twenty years. Tracing those three may be quite a job, even providing you got their names and their old addresses from Gordon—which I doubt very much will happen."

"Appeal to him," Bellew said in a harsh, broken voice.

Warne was thoughtful. "The watch-dog in white Caribbean pants isn't just there to turn away unwelcome callers while the old man's under the weather. A housekeeper could do that. He's a strong-arm boy. Fast on his feet and quick with his fists, bet. And old man Gordon must feel he needs him."

Bellew didn't seem interested. "Maybe he keeps him for company. Look, Warne, I've got to have more, I want the whereabouts of those three men in the Janie Gordon case. Otherwise we don't have a thing."

"Yes, we have," Warne corrected. "I'd know that voice anywhere."

Bellew seemed confused. "What voice?"

"On the phone. The woman. I told you about it."

"Well, then, they're reading my mind," Bellew said, returning to his earlier fear.

Warne made a wry face. "No. No mind reading. I don't think there's any hocus-pocus with a crystal ball, either. But someone has a way of checking on you pretty closely. I figured it might be Mrs. Shafer, so I took her out and tried to find out what she was like. She's the genuine article, and her attitude towards you is tolerant. In fact, almost respectful. You don't hardly find them like that any more."

Bellew licked his lips. "Of course it isn't Mrs. Shafer. She's a nice girl. She's strictly business, and level-headed. She's not a nut writing poison pen letters in her spare time." He thought about it. "Besides, she's too good a typist. An expert. And this other person isn't."

"If I were you," Warne said, "I wouldn't go into a panic. These letter writers are usually timid people. That's why they stay at mail's length. They do their damage at a distance and anonymously because they're scared to get any closer."

To Warne's surprise Bellew at once became even more agitated. He flushed scarlet at the temples, jerked erect, flattened his hands as if ready to jump and bolt. "1 didn't mention this. It seemed so nebulous. But I'm positive someone's sneaking into the office when I'm not around. Perhaps at night. On mornings, before I come in. I've found lights burning, the desk disarranged. The janitress was careless—possibly. Only I don't believe it."

"Well, now you do have a course of action," Warne pointed out. "Start keeping irregular hours. Early and late. Maybe you'll catch him ... or her ... here."

Bellew chewed his lips, his eyes downcast.

Warne said reasonably, "Look, Bellew, this thing with Janie Gordon happened more than twenty years ago. Since then, except for the time when you were out of the business, you've coasted along without any trouble. How many strippers and party girls have you had in your files in that time? Dozens? Hundreds? A couple of thousand? And not one of them was raped and jumped out of a window. They did their job, and collected their pay, and paid your commission, and that was it."

Bellew's lips fluttered. "The letters."

Warne stood up. "It's in your head, Bellew. The guilt and the remorse are tearing you apart. The letters were just a trigger, just a symbol, a reminder. All this time you've rationalized your act in regard to Janie Gordon, and suppressed the guilt, and now you're paying for those years of self-delusion. Get it out into the open and look at it. Unwrap it from the layers of fuzz. Accept your part in the affair, resign yourself to a knowledge of your own mistake. And then turn your mind to other things."

For a moment he thought Bellew was going to break down into tears, and this would have been a good thing, in Warne's opinion.

He was well aware of the studies which had been made of reserved and seemingly emotionless people who kept their boiling on the inside and ended up with stomach cancer. A show of emotion, and in Bellew's case a complete emotional catharsis, was much the healthier course.

But Bellew controlled himself after a moment of indecision. He got to his feet, stiffened his shaking hands, nodded to Warne. "I know you're right, Ed. Everything you've said is on the up and up. I'm just not built to take good advice when I hear it."

At the door, Warne paused. "Promise me this. If the party goes off without incident, you'll ignore any further letters. And if lights are on when you come in in the morning, you'll just turn them off."

Bellew seemed to be looking with haunted eyes across a chasm, on the other side of which was blessed relief. "If the party's successful ... yes."

Still Warne hesitated. "You could pull your girls out of it."

"Not now. Not this late. And besides—"

"I know. You've nerved yourself to face it. And you'd never have that much nerve again."

"Who told you?" Bellew said, with an attempt at his old light humor.

At five o'clock the next evening, Bellew closed his office and went down to the parking lot, got into his car, drove down to Sunset Boulevard and turned west.

The big clubs on the Strip flashed by, the little peaked hills behind them covered with homes and apartment buildings, below and to the left the panorama of West L.A., block upon endless block of homes. Bellew drove with the sun in his eyes, frowning, scarcely seeing any of it. He had to stop for the light at the corner opposite the Beverly Hills Hotel, and as he sat there lost in thought he suddenly said half-aloud, "I'm a pimp." He looked around afterward, as if startled by his own words.

He parked the car in the basement garage and went up in the elevator to his fourth-floor apartment. He went into his living room and dropped his coat on the couch. The room faced the east, so that the light now was soft, brushed with a touch of coming twilight. The room had been furnished by a decorator at Bellew's order. It was quite modern, with Japanese touches—a white couch with black teakwood legs, rattan drapes, a screen framed with bamboo and painted with long-legged black herons. The lights had all been covered with white parchment lanterns. Bellew never came in and looked around but what he felt he must have gotten into the wrong apartment.

He went into the bedroom, then, and shed his coat and tie. Returning to the main room, he turned into the hall which led to the kitchen. He stopped suddenly in his tracks, shut his eyes, and put a hand to his temples as if a pain had struck him there. He waited for a moment or so, weaving a little, and then groped his way to the table and sat down. For several minutes he waited there, and then when the small seizure had passed, the dizziness dying away, he rushed into the front room, to the phone. He looked hurriedly for a name in the phone book, then began to dial. But in the midst of dialing he seemed to run out of energy. He dropped the receiver back into place and sat unmoving on the couch.

"It's no good," he whispered to himself. He rubbed the graying hair back off his forehead, fingered the sideburns absently. "I'm a pimp," he said more loudly into the silence of the room.

The phone rang. Bellew, startled, regarded it as if it were some animate thing clamoring for attention. Finally he lifted the receiver to his ear. "Bellew."

Candy Carroll's voice said, "It's just me here. Checking."

Bellew tried to work his lips, but words didn't come.

"Well. Cat got your tongue?" Candy's voice over the phone was much huskier and sexier than it was otherwise; the receiver picked up the deep rich note, the teasing invitation. "I just wanted you to know where I was staying, so you could mail the check. Remember Chickie? Chickie Anderson? I'm at her place for the time being. Sleeping on her couch."

"I see," Bellew got out stiffly.

"Did I interrupt something? You're awfully quiet. Is there—

someone with you?" The tone insinuated that the someone must be feminine, the situation compromising. Candy couldn't help it; Bellew tried to remind himself of this. That was simply the way her mind worked.

"No one's here. I'll remember to send the check to Miss Anderson's address. Are you all set for tonight?" He waited tensely for her reply.

"Am I ready? What have I got to get ready?" she said drolly.

He wanted to say, watch yourself in the clinches, but knew that this would only amuse her. "I'll keep in touch, I'll let you know when I line up something good," he said.

"You do that."

He hung up the receiver and sat there, wet with sweat, his throat working. Finally he walked back to the kitchen, took a bottle of brandy from a lower cupboard, and returned to the living room. Bellew rarely drank and had a natural resistance to the effect of alcohol. He felt somewhat better, more relaxed now, but not woozy.

Bellew went into the bedroom and started to take off his shoes to lie down, and then his eye fell on his coat over the back of a chair, his tie laid across it. All at once he retied his shoes, put on tie and coat, went back to the front room and picked up his hat, and went out.

He reclaimed his car from the basement garage and headed back the way he had come. At the office building he parked some distance from his allotted space, went into the rear of the building quietly. The halls were shadowy now and re-echoed to his lonely footsteps. He went upstairs making as little noise as possible. He stood outside his office door and listened for a long minute, half-expecting to hear some sound from within. But the building was empty, dead.

He fitted his key into the lock and opened the door. Across the room was Mrs. Shafer's desk, empty, cleared of papers as she always left it, the memo pad and the phone casting a blotch of shadow on the polished surface.

He crossed the outer room and opened the other door. On his

desk the lamp was lit. Bellew saw it as a frightful glow that seemed to explode into his eyes like a burst of stars. He heard his own hoarse cry. And then he caught something more. An odor.

In his confusion and fright he, thought at once of escaping gas, and rushed across the room to open the windows. But even as he fumbled with the lifts of the venetian blinds, his thoughts corrected the error. This wasn't gas, couldn't be—there was nothing here but steam heat.

He stood trembling, clinging to the blind cords, and sniffed the smell and tried to identify it. It was dry, pungent, not unpleasant. It made him think of clean things, stored away. A trunk. A trunk his mother had kept in the attic of their home when he had been a child. Before Bellew's wide, frightened stare some memories billowed: his grandfather's old Army uniform, a flag. A quilt his great-grandmother had pieced. Two little wool suits which had belonged to his brother, who had died at the age of three. Those had been stored away, to keep them safe; and when the trunk lid had been lifted this same smell had drifted forth.

Moth balls.

Bellew stared dazedly about, as if at nightmare. The light cast its round puddle of reflection on the desk. He had turned it out, had most determinedly clicked it off, the last thing before leaving. Not much more than an hour ago.

And someone had come in, had clicked on the light, had left the old faint smell of the trunk, and had gone.

Had gone like a ghost, Bellew thought numbly.

He stumbled over to the desk and searched through the leather file containing phone numbers, and dialed Warne's number at home. The phone rang, but no one answered. Warne wasn't there.

Bellew left the office, locking it. He hadn't switched off the lamp. There didn't seem to be much purpose in doing it. His uninvited caller could come in and switch it on again whenever the mood seized him.

Bellew went home again and tackled the brandy bottle. The liquor reassured him all over again; and he realized whence had come the courage and the uncharacteristic determination to face his enemy. He must be getting drunk. Drunk and brave. With a small grim smile Bellew applied himself to his drinking.

The pain in his head went away. He forgot about his limp. In fact, as he moved about the room he hardly limped at all. The old familiar stiffness faded away, the nerves revived, knitted together, the wound he had suffered on a hunting trip in his early manhood seemed obliterated. He felt almost young again.

He tried to call Warne. No answer.

He found himself growing groggy, and went into the bedroom and lay down. Hours later he roused. He had the beginnings of a hangover and a cold sour taste in his mouth. He sat on the edge of the bed and brushed the fallen hair off his face, and found himself looking at the clock on the bedside commode. Was it past twelve? Really?

Thick fear clogged in his throat. He had to go at once and find out what was happening at the party.

CHAPTER SIX

He found the clubhouse. It was out past Westwood, near a couple of markets and a big department store. The stores were dark, their vast parking lots empty. There were lights inside the low, ranch-style clubhouse, but not much noise, not the joyous racket he had expected.

Instead, the place looked as if an old maids' convention might be going on inside.

Bellew scouted around, keeping to the shadows. There were a lot of big shrubs and a few trees here, and it was all pretty dark. Finally, out in the rear, in the clubhouse parking lot, he discovered what was left of the party. A couple of the girls he had sent out— Candy wasn't with them—and three of the men were drinking out of paper cups and talking together. A light at the top of a standard lit up the scene. There were a half-dozen cars, no more.

One of the men let out a sudden loud guffaw, his humor mixed with explosive indignation. "I don't believe it. Hell, I just don't believe old Joe had any word at all. Straight from headquarters, he said. Going to lower the boom. Did it come off the way he said it would?" The man lowered his jaw like a bull and there were disgruntled murmurs from the others.

"A raid, My God, Joe swore there would be a raid. And so the girls had to dance in their pants. What a frost!"

The second man downed his drink to a chorus of growling agreement.

One of the girls lifted her paper cup mockingly. "I move that old Joe be kicked out of the club!"

"Second it!" A regular chorus answered her. But Bellew scarcely heard this. He realized what had happened, that an alarm had been given by a timid or disapproving member, and that the entertainment committee had gotten cold feet. A relief almost sickening in its intensity flooded through him, and he crept away, mopping his face and neck with a handkerchief.

Nothing had happened to anyone. No one was excited, frenzied by the sight of naked flesh and the assumed look of invitation on the faces of the dancers. No one was out of control, dragging a frightened girl into some dark recess to be violated. These girls were having a last drink before closing up shop. Everyone else had gone home.

He walked softly up into the open veranda and looked into the windows. A couple of elderly men, neatly dressed in business suits, were doing just what he had expected; they were checking an account book and totting up sums of figures on a scratch pad on a table. There had been a party here, all right, but it had been a quiet one. No broken glasses, no torn decorations and burst balloons, and no fallen lodge members sleeping it off under a table.

Again Bellew was conscious of the rush of relief. His flesh quivered and his throat clogged, so that he swallowed, repeatedly and with difficulty. A sudden coolness seemed to brush his skin with dew.

I wish I had a drink, he thought. I wish I had a drink to celebrate with, right now.

Chickie Anderson lived just north of Elysian Park, off Riverside Drive, and the apartment house of four stories sat on the brink of a cut which had been made to enlarge a freeway, On the side where Chickie's windows looked north towards the east end of San Fernando Valley, the drop was more than a hundred feet to the new paving below.

At about four-thirty that morning, before it was completely daylight, a man driving a Volkswagen had to swerve sharply to avoid hitting a body. He parked the little car and ran back, risking being hit by the scattered traffic. Apparently he was the first to notice the girl, the other drivers perhaps in the poor light taking the body to be a bundle of discarded rags. She was wearing a gray satin gown trimmed with black net, over it a negligee of black chiffon. The driver took a good look and saw that she was dead, no mistake about it, and then he looked around dazedly as if searching for a parked car. Where had she come from?

Within a few minutes more cars had stopped and the drivers were out, and a crowd was beginning to form. At this moment a motorcycle cop came roaring up and braked his machine.

A babble of voices answered his request for information. The man who had first stopped tried to sneak away, remembering that his driver's license had expired, and a dozen hands pointed him out, so that it seemed as if he must be guilty of something. The cop demanded to know why he had ditched a dead woman from his car, and the poor man almost fainted.

No one had any idea where the woman had come from. Obviously she had been dropped from a passing car, but no one had noticed it at the time.

The light was growing stronger, and one man, more alert or more curious than the rest, suddenly let out a shout and pointed to the steel link fence at the top of the steep embankment. Fluttering from the top of the wire was a long patch of black chiffon. The cop knelt quickly and straightened the rumpled negligee, and all could see where the fabric had been caught and torn.

"They threw her over the railing!" someone cried.

"Pitched her right over, all right," said a woman in a red shirt and jeans who had a pickup truck with two nanny goats tied in it.

"It's murder, not an accident. She never clumb that way," said an old gardener in his work clothes.

"Maybe she jumped out of the building."

All eyes now searched the towering wall above. On the third floor was an open window from which the screen had been removed, or lost, and out of which white curtains fluttered.

"I'll bet I know what happened," said the stocky woman who owned the goats. "She was out on a Hollywood party all night, drunk, and some wolf after her. And when she woke up afterwards and took a good look at herself she just naturally took a running jump out that window."

There were murmurs in answer, and a bright-eyed man of

about thirty-five drew the woman aside for further conversation. Her theory interested him, since it had the elements of a good story, and he was a newspaper reporter. His name was Fred Robinson. He was tall and rangy and had rusty red hair.

"What's your name?" he asked the woman in the red shirt and jeans.

"Lydia Watkins. I'll tell you something. If that girl there has been out on a farm, tending to animals and working hard, she wouldn't be lying dead in that disgraceful nightgown right now. She'd be milking a goat."

"Milking a goat," Fred Robinson murmured. He was sketching the story now. He loved characters like this, and was far enough in his editor's good graces to be allowed to dress up his stories by quoting them.

"Look at me," said the woman. "I'm almost forty. When I was twenty I had a chance to go like that." She motioned towards the dead girl sprawled on the pavement. "My mother entered my name in a beauty contest. A horrible little man came out to the house. He wanted to measure me. You know how?"

"No. How?"

"Nekkid. Nekkid as the day I was born."

"Your mother wouldn't let you," Fred surmised.

"She chased him with a kettle of boiling water. Him and his tape measure."

"Saved you from ruin," Robinson put in.

"She sure did. And now I'm married and have a little place out the other end of the valley, and ... say, you ever drink goats' milk?"

The cop was using the radiophone on his cycle to call for reinforcements. Traffic had come to a congested halt. People were milling around, staring at the body, and one man was trying to climb the earthen cut to get at the scrap of black chiffon on the fence. Since the cut was almost vertical, he was having a bad time. Fred Robinson got Lydia Watkins' address and hurried back to his car, worked his way free from the tangle and turned into the side street which climbed steeply uphill.

The police had their routine. They would move with cautious

thoroughness. The newspaper man had no such limitations. He took a chance on a wild hunch and went directly to the third floor of the apartment house. A couple of tries drew indignant blanks, and then he rang Chickie's doorbell. Chickie came to the door still half-asleep. She was a small slim girl with an excellent figure, hair bleached platinum this season, and big brown eyes. She slept in a shortie-gown.

"Yes, mister?"

A stab in the dark. "Where's your room-mate?"

Still yawning, she looked behind her. "Candy? Must be in the bathroom. Who're you?"

"Tell her Fred Robinson is here," he said dryly.

She shut the door and he could hear her padding around, and then the door opened again and she was looking out at him. The sleepiness was gone from her eyes and she looked worried. "I can't find her. She must have dressed and gone out."

Still he couldn't be sure, though a sense of jubilance was growing in him. "Check the clothes she wore last night, won't you?"

"That was her party outfit," Chickie pointed out. "But I'll look." She omitted closing the door now, and Robinson stepped in over the sill. He made a lightning-quick survey of the place. It was a typical furnished apartment in the middle-price bracket. Probably about sixty or seventy a month, utilities extra. No linens or dishes. The only wear and tear Chickie would give the kitchen would be mixing drinks in it.

Chickie came out of the bedroom. Her bare legs looked like ivory below the short hem of the gown. "Gosh, I just can't figure it. I don't see a thing missing. It's queer." Her face seemed entirely young and innocent in its bewilderment.

Robinson was over at the open window now. "Come here a minute, will you?"

She stepped close and he gripped her arm and thrust her suddenly at the open drop. She gasped and tried to writhe back, and he said, "Look. Look down there." She looked, forgetting the height and the danger, and in the bright light she must have recognized a friend, for Robinson heard and felt the deep sucking breath she took, getting ready to scream. He jerked her back inside and slapped a hand over her mouth and muffled the yell she let out. "Listen. Screaming won't get you anywhere. The cops will be here pretty soon. Why did you push your chum out of that window?"

He wanted to calm her by the shock of accusation, but it didn't work. As soon as he lifted his hand she screamed, and then she fought free and tore out of the apartment into the hall, still screaming; and all the way down the stairs and into the distance, presumably on her way to the manager. Robinson lit a cigarette and sat in the window sill and smoked calmly. Chickie, in her shortie gown, was certainly going to be a sensation.

What a hell of a break. He had no camera with him.

The cops were with Chickie now, and their attitude towards Robinson, instead of being one of gratitude, was of thinly veiled animosity.

"Scram, louse," said a loose-lipped sergeant of detectives.

"Oh, hell, let him listen," said a coroner's man. "He's just making a living, for Chrissakes."

So Robinson listened.

Chickie was employed at present in one of the local night spots as a strip artist. She had come home at a quarter of two to pick up a swim suit. One of the customers at the club had had cause to celebrate, and had invited the members of the show out to his home, to a combined drink-and-swim fest. When Chickie had come in she had remembered Candy, and in case Candy were already back from the party and sleeping, she had not turned on the lights in the living room.

She had gone into the hall and clicked the light switch there, and by the softened illumination, had looked back to check up on her pal. Candy was under a blanket on the couch. She was wearing the gray satin gown, and the black negligee was laid over a chair.

"Did she wake up while you were home?"

"No. No, she just kept on sleeping." Chickie mopped at her

eyes.

A headline sprang into full-blown life in Robinson's brain.

Last Seen Sleeping....

The story continued. Chickie had stayed at the customer's party until nearly four A.M., when a friend had driven her home. Yes, she remembered the friend's name. She remembered his phone number. She was sure he'd remember dropping her here a little past four o'clock this morning.

The coroner's man said, "That girl has been dead for more than two hours. I'd stake my reputation on it."

Robinson thought, so Chickie has an alibi. He waited for the next question.

"What about this party Miss Carroll attended last night?"

"It was a job," Chickie explained. "You see, Candy was over in Vegas and she couldn't take the heat, being cooped up where it was air-conditioned and not being able to gamble, it just got her down. So Mr. Bellew's, he's her agent, he got her this date for a stag."

"What was she supposed to do at this stag affair?" asked the sergeant.

"Dance," said Chickie, defensively.

"Just dance?"

"She was a good sport," Chickie said. "Maybe they'd have asked for something extra. She'd have done it. That's the way Candy was."

"Maybe something had happened to her at that party," said the sergeant, his eyes moist.

Robinson said silently, you bastard, you're raping her right now in that filthy mind of yours. He thought of the soft pearly flesh sprawled on the freeway, the disarranged gown, the transparent negligee.

Robinson found a phone book and looked up Bellew's name and address. It was still too early for the man to be at his office, but Robinson had a hunch that if he went to the apartment house where Bellew lived, he'd collide with a regiment of cops.

Maybe he could bribe a janitor to let him in the office, he decided. He drove to the address just off Sunset, parked at the curb, and went in. It wasn't yet eight o'clock and the place was deserted.

He found a stocky, gray-haired man putting trash into cans at the rear door. For five dollars the man shook his head and for ten he merely looked mildly interested. But twenty produced a key.

"You're on your own, buster," he warned Robinson. "If anybody squawks I'll say the key was swiped."

"I'll only be a minute."

He went up to the second floor and inserted the key in the lock. The office inside looked about what he had expected. The big photos of movie personalities were phonies, of course, dolled up with forged signatures to make the place look like MCA or Famous Artists. He crossed the outer room, opened the door, noted the lighted lamp on the desk and then took a good look at the display around the walls. Robinson whistled.

Then a new idea occurred to him. He made a swift survey of the nude display and found a picture he was sure resembled Candy Carroll. No one was going to complain about a minor mistake, anyway. He detached the glossy picture from its holdings and tucked it away in an inner pocket.

He was busily rummaging in Bellew's desk when he heard a sound from the outer room. He froze, alert and watchful. The inner door opened and a big guy stood there, something angry and disgusted in his face. Robinson noted a badly scarred eyebrow and a spilled-eggyolk tie, plus a suit that didn't exactly fit though it was hard to say why.

"Your time's up, brother," said the newcomer. "You've just made the last delivery. The poison pen postal service is going out of business." He crossed the room in two long jumps and grabbed Robinson and slammed him against the wall.

Robinson thought dazedly, hell, he acts as if he knew me. But I never saw this character in my life, up to now. Then his mind, trained to pick up every unlikely scrap, reverted to something the big man had said. *The poison pen postal service....*

Even as he ducked the blows aimed at him by the big character in the egg-yolk tie, Robinson thrilled with a hunch that he was onto something good. From a dead girl sprawled on the freeway, to the office where she was listed as a client, to a dust-up over something about poison pen letters—who could ask for anything more?

CHAPTER SEVEN

Robinson patted his swelling eye with a damp handkerchief while he dialed a number on Bellew's phone. "Hello, Katy. Give me rewrite."

Across the room Warne stared ruefully at his skinned knuckles. He had begun to realize that he had done Bellew the opposite of a favor. Candy Carroll was dead, having apparently jumped out of a high window, and now thanks to him this reporter had wind of the letters which had prophesied just such an occurrence.

Robinson rattled off the details of Candy's last hours. When he had replaced the phone in its cradle, Warne said, "How about giving Bellew a break? He's a decent little old guy and you've got him in a position to crucify him."

Robinson patted his temple and grinned. "I don't make or give breaks, buddy. I just write the facts as I see 'em. Candy Carroll took a flying leap out of a window. It would seem she had something unpleasant on her mind at the time. Now, Bellew had sent her out on a party job. I've got to find out what happened at that party, how rough it got, and maybe what the lodge brothers insisted poor little Candy do for them."

Warne looked disgusted. "She was an old hand, a professional."

"I'm also interested in the business about the letters," Robinson went on dryly. "You feel like talking about it?"

"Someone's been heckling Bellew about his business, that was all." Damned if this nosy reporter would get out of him the story of Janie Gordon and Bellew's long years of repressed guilt.

Robinson nodded, his eyes thoughtfully fixed on Warne. "It's a business that sort of lends itself to heckling, don't you think? A lot of people have very strict ideas in regard to amusement. And a guy in a business like this one could make a mistake without half trying." He paused as if to consider the possibilities. Under the rusty red thatch, Warne realized, was a sharp and knowing mind. "Or has Bellew had some definite piece of bad luck in the past?"

Let him dig it out of the newspaper morgue, Warne thought to himself. He tried to keep any hint of knowledge or alarm out of his face.

"How long have you known him?" Robinson asked.

"Oh, four or five years anyway. I opened an office next to his, here, when. I got out of the Army. We sort of gradually got acquainted."

"Run around together?"

"No. After office hours I go my way and he goes his. He's a pretty quiet type, by the way. He books them but he doesn't play them."

Robinson stretched his legs behind Bellew's desk. "Ever meet this Candy Carroll?"

"I think so. Not long ago, in this office. At least, the description you give fits her. I didn't speak, just took a long look."

Robinson nodded. "I'll bet."

Warne said, "Look, I'm sorry I jumped you. If you'll go to a doctor with that eye, I'll foot the bill."

Robinson jeered, "Well, that's mighty decent of you!"

"I'm not trying to be smart. I've already apologized for the mistake. Bellew said someone's been snooping here, leaving the letters, and so when I saw you—"

"Forget it," Robinson interrupted. "Now, do you know anything about this party last night? Where it was, who held the wingding?"

"You'll have to find that out from Bellew," Warne said. "All I know is that he was hoping it would come off okay."

The wrong thing to say—Robinson pounced on it eagerly. "Oh? Any reason it shouldn't?"

Warne shrugged. "Oh, these letters had him rattled. Perhaps I shouldn't be telling you about them—it's really his business—but since I made a fool of myself by jumping you, I felt I ought to explain."

Robinson got out of Bellew's chair and walked around restlessly, looking at the nude display on the walls. "I have a hunch, buddy. I have a hunch you know a lot more than what you're telling me."

He shot a quick glance over his shoulder. "You're trying to cover for Bellew because you know him and like him. But I've a feeling he sent this girl into a mess last night. And sometime early this morning she decided she didn't like what she had to do for a living. And so she took that first big step, the step that's such a lulu."

"Thinking is your privilege," Warne said smoothly, "but excuse me if I don't listen any longer. I've got work to do."

He left Robinson musing over the naked ladies and went back to his own office. He shut the door and turned the latch, went directly to the desk and took the telephone off the receiver and dialed Mrs. Shafer's home.

Her voice was cool, distinct and hurried. She seemed pleased when she realized who it was, but when Warne suggested that she come down to Bellew's office at once, she demurred.

"I'm due to leave for class right now. I have to drop Dotty at Aunt Faye's and literally run."

"One of Bellew's dancers jumped out of a window last night," Warne said. "There's going to be some ugly publicity, since the jumping must have followed almost immediately after a date Bellew arranged for her."

She cried out, shocked, "Oh, that's dreadful!"

"The cops and the newspaper reporters are going to run you down for questioning this morning, either at school or at your other afternoon job. It occurred to me that it might be better all around if you were to meet them here. You'll be at the scene of operations, with the files to refer to in case you can't answer any of their questions."

She thought it over. "Yes, you're right. I don't want any such circus going on around Dotty. Or stirring up Aunt Faye." There was a sudden gasp. "Oh, heavens, I don't want Aunt Faye to know anything about it. She's been beating the subject to death."

"Unless you can keep her away from the newspapers and the news broadcasters, you'll have some trouble."

Sandra made a rueful sound over the wire: "She gobbles up soap operas. There must be bits of news she hears now and then. Oh, it's silly to worry over what she'll say. I'll just try to ignore it."

"When will you be here?"

"Right away. As soon as I can drop Dotty and head for Sunset Boulevard."

Warne went back to Bellew's office. The newspaper man was gone and the door was locked. Warne returned to his own place and tried to work, but the effort was useless. When he heard heels tapping in the hall, he left his desk again and went out. When he saw what was coming towards him, his jaw dropped.

Mrs. Shafer, looking cowed and almost tearful was in the lead. Behind her, stiff as a ramrod in the unadorned black dress was Aunt Faye. She had the air of a vice squad invading a brothel. Or of Carrie Nation with her sharp little hatchet. She marched with a foot-slapping sound, *whomp whomp whomp*. When she got even with Warne she gave him a frosty smile and said, "Thank you, sir. You did my niece a favor."

Sandra Shafer got her keys from her purse and opened Bellew's door. Warne followed the two women inside. He felt somehow that Sandra needed protection from the fierce old woman. She was too loyal and affectionate to rebuff Aunt Faye for her browbeating. Perhaps he could put in a tactful word or two.

And perhaps get his head snapped off for his trouble, he added to himself.

Aunt Faye looked all around the outer office. She goggled at the photos of the stars on the walls. "He knows these people?"

"Hardly," said Warne. "It's just display, something to dress up the place and make it look properly theatrical."

"Well, I never." With a rush, she hurried to the inner door and snapped it back and stood, stricken speechless, glaring in at the tier-on-tier of naked smiling girls around the walls.

She caught her breath at last. "They're ... they're ..."

"They sure are," said Warne over her shoulder. "Every last one of them. And besides, they can dance. Or at least a little."

She must have heard the jeer behind his words for she stiffened in anger. Then a cold bleak ruthlessness gleamed in her eyes. She marched into Bellew's inner sanctum and put her big black alligator bag on his desk, stripped off black cotton gloves, and went to the wall and began ripping down the pictures.

"Wait a minute!" Warne cried in dismay.

She looked at him over her outstretched arm, her face sharp as a hatchet. "Stop and think, Mr. Warne. When the police and reporters get here there'll be a lot of prowling around. They won't stay in that outer office. There will be pictures taken, and impressions formed and put down in words. This place will have a glare of publicity on it to shame a movie premiere. And my niece will be in the middle of it." She pursed her lips as if waiting for him to catch on. "Won't it look much better for Sandra—not to mention this man Bellew—if there isn't a display like this one?"

She was right. Warne thought admiringly, she was a smart old cookie. The newspaper photographers would have made a holiday in here. And some nasty suppositions would have been printed about Sandra and Bellew.

Warne set to work and Sandra followed. They stripped the walls of the nude photos, stacking them on Bellew's desk; and then Warne took them all into his own office and locked them in a file cabinet. Old Aunt Faye found a bottle of cleaning fluid and a rag in Bellew's office closet, and scrubbed off all the marks left by the tape on the painted walls.

As she rubbed, Aunt Faye muttered, "Thank God I left Dotty with the landlady and came here with Sandra."

"Amen," said Warne.

In the outer office with Sandra, he tried to prepare her for what must come. "The cops won't be the worst. They'll ask questions, some of them insulting, but they'll at least listen to your answers. The reporters will try to put words in your mouth. That's what you have to look out for."

She nodded, then glanced at him a little helplessly. She wore the horn-rims, and had her hair pulled back trimly, and her black skirt and plain white blouse looked very business-like.

Aunt Faye came out, putting on her gloves. "I'm leaving now. I don't care to be caught here by these snooping police. Call me when you're ready to pick up Dotty tonight."

"Thanks, Aunt Faye. Thank you for everything," said Sandra.

"And I take back every word I didn't say," Warne added.

Warne was in his own office, when the cops arrived. He didn't want to be around to fend off questions, perhaps to let slip something about Bellew's mysterious letter writer who had, it seemed, been able not only to read Bellew's mind but to forecast the future.

Warne was quite curious about that party last night, and was trying to think of a way he could get information, when he remembered a trick he'd used during his college days. Sometime during that last frantic talk, Bellew had dropped a name, the title of the outfit, giving the wingding at which Candy Carroll was to appear. What had it been? Business Men's something-or-other. He picked up the phone book and leafed through the yellow pages to Fraternal Organizations. He found it there: Business Men's All-America Patriots. Now who thought that up, he wondered, as he dialed.

A woman's crisp voice said, "Church and Company. Miss Ragsdale speaking."

Warne said, "I must have the wrong number. I'm looking for the All-America Patriots."

"Oh. We accept messages for the organization," said Miss Ragsdale, "since our President, Mr. Church, is one of the directors." She paused, then added: "May I take a message?"

"My name is Dr. Thorne. I have a patient who is a member and who attended a party last night. I wanted to talk to some other member about what was served there in the way of food and drink. It's pretty serious."

Her voice warmed up immediately. "Oh, I see. Just hold on, doctor, and I'll contact Mr. Church."

Mr. Church came on the wire finally. He sounded small, fat and pompous. "This is Church speaking. You're a physician?"

"Dr. Edward Thorne." Before Mr. Church could ask further questions, such as where his office was located and who was sick and what hospital they'd been taken to, Warne rushed on. "I have a pretty sick man on my hands. He thinks he might have eaten or drunk something at the party last night which disagreed with him. Can you help me?"

"Well … sorry to hear … as a matter of fact, though—" Mr. Church was picking his words cautiously, as if perhaps they were being written down somewhere.

Warne laughed in as worldly a manner as he could summon. "I guess you boys really hung one on, hmmm? I hear you even had entertainers."

"Ah … ah—"

"Well, I guess boys will be boys, especially when the cat's away, if I may mix a metaphor or two. How were those strippers? Always wanted to catch an act like that. You got your money's worth, I'll bet." All the time Warne was speaking he could hear Mr. Church growing more and more agitated, sputtering words and making small moans. Perhaps he thought Miss Ragsdale was listening. And perhaps Miss Ragsdale was a chum of Mrs. Church.

"You must understand … doctor, you must positively understand that there was no rough or vulgar performance of any sort at our little get-together." Desperation caused Mr. Church to speak quickly and emphatically. "The dancers did not strip. They put on a small entertainment, fully clothed. As for the food and drink, I can refer you to the caterers." There was a papery rattling as if Mr. Church searched for the caterer's name among the files on his desk. In a gasping tone he read it then aloud to Warne. "They can tell you exactly what was served. Shrimp, I remember. Shrimp in a gooey sauce. Chicken—I didn't try it. The drinks seemed fine. I had … ah … just a little wine."

You old hypocrite, Warne said silently. He put a lot of surprise into his voice. "There certainly must have been a radical change of plan."

In his agitation Mr. Church forgot to wonder why a doctor was curious about the other details of the affair. "There certainly was a change," he said, biting off the words, "Since one of our members declared we were due to have a raid."

"And nobody danced naked?"

Mr. Church yelped, "Certainly not!" and must have instantly transferred the call, for next came Miss Ragsdale saying sweetly, "Will there be anything else, doctor?"

"I think I have everything I need," he said politely, and hung up.

If Church were to be believed—and somehow Warne did believe him—Candy Carroll had pranced around at an affair resembling a rather late-hour Sunday-school picnic. Afterwards, struck with shame, she'd taken her life by jumping out of a window. Like Janie Gordon who had been raped at seventeen.

Warne sat shaking his head over it. It didn't make sense.

CHAPTER EIGHT

Warne had work which demanded attention; he had come earlier than usual today in order to get it done. Now he deliberately forced his thoughts away from the provocative puzzle of Candy's death, and settled down to the job. He dictated a batch of letters and reports into his office machine for later transcription by the public stenographer downstairs.

At about eleven-thirty he knocked off, went next door and looked in on Sandra. She was at the desk, alone. She looked tired and exasperated, but when she saw Warne she smiled wanly. "How did it go?" Warne asked.

"The way you said it would. But I think I held my own." She leaned back in her chair, fluffing the hair off her neck with her fingers, and her full well-shaped breasts pushed out inside the trim cotton blouse. "The police seemed determined to prove that Mr. Bellew had some sort of agreement about Miss Carroll, that she would be available for what they called 'other services' after the entertainment at the party was over. I had to scotch that, but quick." She smiled at him again, her glance warming. "You'll never know how glad I am Aunt Faye got rid of those pictures."

"No flies on her," Warne agreed, "even if she is a bit of an alarmist."

"She's just a little old-fashioned," Sandra said.

"I'm going out for coffee," Warne added. "Want to come along?"

In the little cafe down the block, Warne ordered coffee for both of them, then turned to the girl. "What about the reporters?"

"There were two of them. They didn't give me as hard a time as I had expected. I think they took one look and decided I wasn't the type they needed to liven up the press."

Warne put a hand over hers on the counter between them. "I guess I had some sort of idea like that. But now I'm beginning to notice things I never saw before."

Her eyes dropped and a small smile touched her lips.

A newsboy came in off the street and Warne hurriedly bought a paper, spreading it on the counter where he and Sandra could read it. Candy's death was front page news. Warne read the headline: *Last Seen Sleeping*. He read on and found the account of the interview with Chickie.

In a second statement to police, Warne read, Chickie had supplied further details. "I was very much surprised to find Candy home so early," Chickie was quoted. "Usually she got in much later from a party like that one. Sometimes, even, the next morning! Those Patriot guys must be a very quiet bunch of fellows."

Warne grinned to himself. Mr. Church and his fellow lodge members had some fast footwork cut out for them at home, explaining the presence of a girl like Candy Carroll at their party.

The paper explained that Chickie's whereabouts during the night were fully accounted for. There was no question that she was not to blame for Candy's dive through the window: The host at the swimming party had been chasing Chickie in the pool at about the time Candy had died.

The obvious conclusion, according to the reporters, was that the stripper had committed suicide during a moment of uncharacteristic depression.

"It's crazy," Warne muttered over his coffee.

Sandra had been reading, too. "I wouldn't have said she was the kind of girl to get into such a mood. She gave off an air of being satisfied with herself."

"Yes, I thought so, too."

Lower on the page was an interview with the landlady. She gave Chickie Anderson an excellent character. Chickie was a quiet, decent girl and if her job happened to keep her in an atmosphere of rowdy sex, she certainly didn't bring it home with her. She'd had her present apartment for nearly two years and there wasn't a nicer tenant in the building. The landlady hadn't met Miss Carroll, since she was simply a temporary guest of Miss Anderson's. The landlady had found the missing screen off the window, however—on the ground just inside the steel link fence at the top of the freeway embankment. The frame of the screen was all broken apart by its fall from the high window. And the screening itself was almost completely bulged out and torn from the frame as if by strong pressure from within. "She just jammed it out bodily," the landlady was quoted as saying. "In a hurry to hop out and get it over with, I guess."

Warne was frowning, his mouth tight-lipped. "Now, that screen is interesting."

"Well, she must have jumped out in the dark," Sandra replied, "and so just didn't see that there was a screen in the way." She gave him a quick anxious glance. "It couldn't be anything but suicide, could it?"

"I don't know." Warne was thinking to himself that Candy's death certainly made Bellew's mysterious letter writer into a first class prophet. "Has Bellew called you this morning?" he asked of Sandra.

"No, I haven't heard from him. Probably it didn't occur to him I might come in, and besides, he'd be busy. The police must have grilled him thoroughly about his dealings with Miss Carroll."

"We'd better check up on him." Warne rose, paid the bill and took Sandra back outdoors. The morning was warming up and below them, a half-block away, Sunset Boulevard was busy with traffic. Warne noticed a blue Cadillac coupe swing off and turn their way. He and Sandra had almost reached the door of their own building when Warne took a second and closer look at the car. Abruptly, he jerked Sandra around, held her as if they were studying the display in a small shop window.

She was a quick-witted girl. She made no move to look back at the passing car. "What is it?" she asked softly.

"Someone I know." He waited tensely. The Cadillac went by slowly, and the couple in it appeared to be reading street numbers, searching for a certain address. There was no mistaking the man, Warne decided, not even in the pale and distorted image reflected in the shop window. Native Boy's lean and deeply tanned face, topped by the almost snow-white butch cut, was too distinctive to be confused with anyone else. He'd had a very brief glimpse of the girl with him; she was small, as young at least as Mr. Gordon's watchdog. A pert face. Black hair cut short with bangs, the style girls called a Dutch bob.

"I think I've seen that man before," Sandra said, looking at the reflection on the glass.

Warne was keeping his own head bent, hoping that the man in the Cad wouldn't recognize him. "Where?"

"I can't remember." Her tone was puzzled as well as surprised. "Is he a client of yours?"

"Not exactly. He works for a man I interviewed not long ago. Let's go on." The car was up at the other end of the block, making a U-turn. Warne and Sandra went into the empty lobby of their own building and up the stairs.

"We were going to call Mr. Bellew," she reminded.

There was no need to call, though. The outer door was open and Bellew was inside. He had crossed to the inner door and opened it, and now stood in the open doorway staring in a dazed way at the walls where the nude ladies had once cavorted. Hearing Warne and Sandra come in, he turned around. The effort to brace himself, to control his emotions, was visibly almost too much for him. Then, recognizing who it was, he brightened a little. "Oh. It's you, Warne. And Mrs. Shafer—I can't tell you how grateful I am that you came in. I heard about it from one of the reporters."

"I was glad to help," she said quickly. "I'm terribly sorry about what happened to Miss Carroll."

Warne said, "Mrs. Shafer's aunt came down with her, and had the bright idea to remove those fascinating pictures."

"That was wise." Bellew seemed to make an effort to look less gloomy.

Warne went on, "I think you might as well discuss those letters in front of Mrs. Shafer. She's been on the firing line for you all morning."

"I suppose ... Yes, it's all right."

They sat down and Warne spent a few minutes outlining Bellew's troubles with the poison pen writer. Sandra was at first surprised and confused, but soon grew indignant. "I wish you had told me about them before this," she said to Bellew. "Perhaps I could have helped. I'd have kept my eyes open for anything significant."

"It doesn't matter now," said Bellew in a tired, dwindling voice.

Sandra said sympathetically, "I'm simply astonished, Mr. Bellew, that you were able to carry on. It must have been dreadful. But then—this I don't understand at all, how could this person who seemed just to want to persecute you, foretell what was actually going to happen?"

"He ... he *made* it happen!" Bellew blurted, as though the words were torn out of him. Then he shook his head and half-collapsed in the chair, rubbing his face between his hands. "I don't know what I'm saying," he protested. "Don't pay any attention to me."

Warne's voice had an edge of anger. "I think you might have something there. Don't disparage it."

Sandra was staring at Warne. Bellew had lifted his bloodshot eyes.

Warne Went on quickly: "Don't you see, it's just too pat? It came out too neatly? You got the warnings, you were nervous and scared, you were prepared for the worst—and the worst went right ahead and happened? To put it bluntly—this thing stinks."

Bellew licked his lips. No hope glimmered behind the suffering mask of his face.

"Perhaps it's just a strange coincidence," Sandra murmured.

"It's not a coincidence at all. And I'm damned if I believe Candy Carroll jumped out of a window so a prophecy might come true. So that leaves just one other possibility." He faced Sandra's worried gaze and Bellew's draggingly ill one. "Murder."

The word had a flat, hollow ring in the silence of the office. It was a moment before he got any reaction from Bellew, and then the older man merely shook his head wearily.

"You've got to tell the police about the letters," Warne pointed out. "They need to know. It's part of the picture."

Bellew's face worked, his mouth quivering as he sought to form words with his lips. "They'll cut me to pieces!" he got out.

"Forget about any chance of being blamed for what happened to Janie Gordon," Warne insisted. "That's ancient history now. You have a client dead, a girl whose career you managed—"

"No. No!" Bellew seemed almost incoherent. He stood up before his chair and pounded on the desk. "I won't tell the police! I refuse to do any such thing. It would be utter madness. They'd have me locked up and the key thrown away before I could blink."

He fell back into the chair, and stillness settled again in the room. Sandra seemed embarrassed by Bellew's frantic cowardice. Warne, having talked to him previously, was less surprised. The old affair of Janie Gordon had left a sensitive spot in Bellew's makeup, probably a sense of guilt, in Warne's opinion, which had festered through the years. He wasn't a logical thinking human being in that direction.

As if ashamed of his outburst, Bellew tried to talk in an ordinary tone. "Besides, there's this angle. The Janie Gordon case has nothing to do with Candy's death. No matter whether it was suicide—or the other. I thought yesterday—as I told you—that I was sending Candy and the three other girls to much the same kind of party Janie Gordon had been sent to. But I was wrong."

Warne wondered how Bellew had acquired the information so quickly. But Bellew's next words enlightened him.

"I was restless last night. Unsettled. I kept remembering the Gordon affair, and those damned letters. I drank a little brandy, tried to pass the time, finally lay down and tried to sleep. But in the end I had to go and see what was happening. I went out to the clubhouse and saw for myself, listened to the members talking—someone had tipped off the entertainment committee that if they staged a nude show a police raid would be pulled on them."

"That must have relieved your mind," Warne put in.

"Immensely. I can't express how I felt. But the point I want to emphasize is this. Candy wasn't at a rowdy shindig where anything unpleasant could have happened to her. I'll bet it was the tamest evening she'd spent in years."

"You didn't see her out there?"

"She'd already gone home."

"If she jumped out of the window, then," Warne said musingly, "it had nothing to do with the job you sent her on. It. was because of something else entirely."

In spite of his own convictions, Warne was half convinced. It would be history's craziest happenstance, if it had happened this way. But who was he to say that it was impossible?

Bellew, much calmer now because he seemed to have Warne agreeing with him, went on. "There's another item which shows that Candy's death is totally outside this other pattern. Yesterday in my worry I came back to the office almost as soon as I reached home. Someone had already slipped in here, lit the desk lamp, and gone out. And left a distinct smell so I wouldn't miss the fact of their presence."

"What sort of smell?" Warne demanded.

"Moth balls."

There was a moment of silence and then Sandra said, "What was that? *Moth balls?*"

"Yes, that's what it was. I couldn't have been mistaken. Moth balls." Bellew pressed the point home with firmness.

"Look at it this way," Bellew said in his exhausted voice. "The tricks, the persecution, must still be going on. At the time the office was prowled, Candy was getting ready for the club date. Would anyone piddle around leaving a lamp lit and spreading a smell of moth balls—when he had such a hell of a vengeance as Candy's suicide all set up for the next few hours?"

It sounded logical. Logical as hell. Warne admitted it to himself, but not to Sandra or to Bellew. He had a strange feeling that if they deluded themselves far enough in this direction, one of Bellew's taloned specters would tap them on the back.

CHAPTER NINE

Fred Robinson pushed aside his ham-on-rye and bent over his beer. He felt pensive and dissatisfied. He had given his best, and somehow it lacked the flavor of completion. He'd written the story on Candy Carroll and it was being set up now for the afternoon editions. Along with the glossy picture he'd stolen off Bellew's wall.

But the job was done now, and to his unhappiness it wasn't enough.

A stripper diving out of a high window is only a one-day's wonder, a twenty-four hours' sensation. He tried to remember this, to quiet the restlessness inside him; but it didn't work. There ought to be more.

When he finished the beer he followed it with a quick shot of whiskey and then went out, got into his car, and drove back to the apartment house where Chickie Anderson lived. He parked, climbed the stairs to the lobby, and used the self-service elevator, getting out on the-floor below Chickie's. He rang several bells before getting an answer. Obviously most of the tenants were by now out at work.

The woman he finally got was a heavy-set, faded blonde, around forty, wearing a red checked gingham house dress, who put her hand over her mouth to yawn even as she opened the door a crack to peek out at him.

He flashed his best smile. "Hope I didn't interrupt a nap."

"In five minutes, you would have."

"I'm a reporter." He dug out his identification, meanwhile sizing her up. "I guess you know about the excitement around here early this morning."

She shook her head. "Hot damn, I'll say I heard about it. Her apartment's right over my head. Them cops got feet like pile drivers. You think they'd stop and consider, somebody might be trying to snatch forty winks downstairs? Nuts. Nuts, I say."

He assumed a slightly wistful air. "Well, I guess there isn't much more anybody could tell us. It's all been hashed over."

"Not here, it hasn't." She widened the crack between door and lintel. "You want to come in? I could offer a drink if you take gin with orange pop."

He had learned long ago to take what was offered. "Right down my alley." He smiled again, and she must have thought his glance admiring, for she smoothed the gingham over her hips and pursed her lips a little. Robinson looked around. "Say, you've got a cute place here. Fixed up better than the rest of them, those I've seen."

"It's my hobby."

She was a crepe paper artist. There were crepe paper flowers in about a half-dozen vases in the room, a paper parrot in an imitation bird cage made of paper-wrapped wire, and a big paper monkey, brown with a dusty white face, hanging from the imitation mantle.

On the way to the kitchen, she paused to point to the monkey. "I made him first, when I was just beginning. Tail's too long."

"He's fine." Robinson added to himself: what you need in here, baby, is a nice hot bonfire. Robinson sat down and found something tickling the back of his head, and looked back to meet the eyes of a crepe-paper cobra sticking up out of a brown paper basket on a table behind the chair. For an instant Robinson almost choked with fright.

She came back with the drinks in her hands, two gin and orange pop without even the saving grace of ice cubes. One she shoved into his hand.

She stood in the middle of the floor and spraddled her legs a little as if bracing herself for a blow below the belt. She lifted the glass and said, "Cheers!" and then downed about half the mixture, and then stood blankly, waiting to hear from headquarters.

Robinson said, "Likewise," and tipped the glass enough so that he could stick his tongue into the liquid and taste it. Mostly pop, he decided.

She sat down and patted her faded hair and said, "There was

some horrible laughing went on up there during the night. A regular hyena act."

It took a moment for it to register; he was slow to catch that she was giving him something utterly new. Then he said, "You've told this to the police?"

"I hadn't remembered till just now," she said coyly.

He was instantly suspicious. Flattered by his attention, she must be making it up. He said guardedly, "Funny how a person's memory can improve all at once like that."

"Nothing funny about it, not a goddam thing. If they had asked nice, I might have remembered earlier."

"Oh, you've got to make allowances for cops," Robinson explained. "Do you mind telling me about this laughter you heard?"

"It was loud," she said, with an air of genuinely calling something back to mind. "It was loud and not very funny. You know what I mean? Somebody laughs at a joke, it's one way, it's kind of like this. Ha, ha, ha."

"Ha, ha, ha," Robinson echoed, trying to get the exact shade of meaning she'd put into it.

Robinson said, "Now this laughter you heard from the apartment upstairs—it was different, right?"

"Hot damn, was it different! It wasn't even out of the same bottle. It was mean. Nasty. Like maybe, you see somebody forget and put his pipe in his pocket and catch his pants on fire. Like this. Hee, hee, hee."

"Hee, hee, hee," Robinson repeated solemnly. "By the way, I ... auh ... I forgot to get your name. And I'll need it for the paper."

She stuck up her chin a little. "I'm Mrs. Marion Hackendyke. Married. Thirty-nine years old. Have two kids. Boy's in the Army, Signal Corps, girl's married and lives in Oakland. No grandchildren, yet." She peered at him anxiously.

"Fine, Fine. Now—when was all this laughing going on upstairs? Did you notice the time?"

"I sure did. I woke up and waited a while, and when it went on, I looked at the clock, and I hollered out the window, 'What in the hell's so funny at three o'clock in the morning? Goddam you, shut up!' And they shut."

"A man?"

"Woman. I figure it was that Miss Carroll, the stripper up there visiting overnight with the other one."

"You'd heard her laugh before?"

"No, I hadn't. Of course it could have been some other woman if another woman had come in."

"Did you hear any conversation?"

Marion Hackendyke shook her head firmly. "Not a word."

"Then it could have been—not too likely, but perhaps—it could have been Miss Carroll laughing over something to herself. Hysterical, maybe."

Marion thought about it, looking, at the pale orange drink in her hand. "Might have been. If she was going off her rocker. And I guess she did flip or she'd have never took that flying jump out the window."

"I guess that's what she was getting ready to do," Robinson assured her.

Marion was somewhat disappointed; he could see that. "Here I thought maybe I had a clue, or something."

"Don't be discouraged. I'll use this little detail, never fear."

He pried around, but she recalled nothing more. When she wanted to give him another orange pop and gin, he rose to leave; and when she tried to press the paper monkey on him as a gift souvenir, he fled. He went downstairs to the manager's apartment and rang the bell.

The landlady was a small compact woman with a brown mole on her cheek; fuzzy slightly pink hair, and a smell of soap. When Robinson had explained who he was and asked wistfully for any additional scraps of information, she took him down into the basement store-room and showed him the broken window screen. He made arrangements for a photographer to call and make pictures of it, and then left.

He wanted to talk to Chickie Anderson, too; but he had made up his mind to look her up at work. Chickie's working dress would have much more reader appeal, he figured, than even the shortie nightgown of her leisure hours. He made a mental note to be sure to take the camera with him.

Warne was behind his desk, at work, when Native Boy walked in without even the preamble of a knock. No Caribbean pants today. He wore a soft gray shirt and a cream-colored tropical suit, very sharp, and a Panama hat with a green silk band and a tiny yellow feather in the bow. Warne looked up and said, "Hello. Where's your girl friend?"

Native Boy drew his lips back off his strong white teeth in a grimace that in no way resembled a smile. "So that *was* you, standing by the shop window hiding your face. What's the matter? Bashful? Avoiding friends?" He came towards Warne on the balls of his feet and Warne smelled trouble in the room, an odor as crackling as if a brush fire were raging towards him across his patch of green carpet.

Warne put down the pencil and pushed the scratch pad away, and stood up.

The deep blue eyes in the darkly tanned face studied Warne for a moment. "You fought once. Maybe eight, ten years ago. You haven't fought much since. You got the eyebrow from a cut above the eye. You learned a little something from it. But you haven't practiced lately." He gave Warne the shark's mealtime smile again. "I practiced yesterday. Two hours in the gym."

Warne turned his head questioningly. "With Mr. Gordon?"

"Mr. Gordon's my employer. I wouldn't use him for a punching bag." The fists below the cream-colored sleeves tightened, the knuckles paling on the deeply tanned flesh. "You look like you expect me to jump you."

"Come on," Warne invited. "Hell, I can only die once."

He saw the slightly squatting posture, and sensed the steel springs in the massive legs. Native Boy came at him like a truck with attached hammers, but Warne made no move to put up his fists in his defense. He waited until the younger man made his rush and then stuck a knee into his groin, grabbed his arm and with a wrenching, crippling toss he flung Native Boy over his shoulder against the wall. The whole building quivered.

Warne bent above the prone body. "I haven't fought for almost ten years. They teach you a substitute in the Army. And I got awfully good at Judo."

The man on the floor made sucking and gargling sounds as his flattened lungs fought for air. The blue eyes stared glassily up at Warne as if he were hovering in a fog. "I like to know the names of people who come calling," Warne said. He flipped open the cream-colored jacket and riffled through the pockets for a wallet. The one he found was Morocco, initialled in gold. There was about four hundred dollars, more or less, in the money bank. Warne dug for the driver's license. "James Terence Gordon. Nice name. Initials J.T.G. All proper, all accounted for. Now let's see. You're either a relative, or adopted. Say twenty-two or twenty-three, you'd have been born about the time Mr. Gordon's daughter killed herself. He and his wife could have been lonely, could have taken in a kid."

James Gordon wasn't in condition to answer. Warne got him on a chair, doused him with water from the cooler.

"You're a mess, boy," Warne commiserated, pouring water on the white butch cut and watching sympathetically as it dribbled down the coat.

"You ... son of a bitch—" James labored over the words as if he were learning a foreign language. "Soon ... as I get my wind ... I'm going to tear you to pieces ... little—pieces."

"Now, that's not a nice thing to say," Warne corrected. "Here I am, working over you to revive you. I think ... yes, I think I'd better call the cops."

A certain savage withdrawal stiffened the figure in the chair.

"Don't like that idea?" Warne wondered. "Don't crave coppers? Why did you come calling with your mitts up, anyway? It's not the sociable style." He brought more water, and James flinched and gasped under the icy touch, and tried to push Warne away. Warne let him have the whole cupful in the face. "Perhaps Mr. Gordon had a sudden improvement of memory. Perhaps he recalled the name of the man I described to him."

"Bellew," James got out with a sucking gasp. "Bellew sent you."

"Oh, you know that? Well, this simplifies everything. We can get down to cases. Why did Gordon send you here to beat me up?"

There was tight-lipped silence from James Gordon.

Warne yanked down the back of the coat over the chair, pinioning James Gordon's arms, and then slapped him hard. "You've got a hard face but I can soften it. Why did Gordon send you?"

The voice came out angry and grating. "To see if you were who you said you were. That's all." A red mark flamed on his cheek where Warne's slap had landed.

"Since I was just an insurance adjustor, after all, you felt free to belt me around a little. Or maybe a lot. So I'd stay away from Mr. Gordon and keep my nose out of his affairs." Warne stared into the ferocious blue eyes with their promise of future violence. "What's he got to cover up? Why does he need you?"

He dug his fingers into the butch cut and gripped the short hair and jerked James's face up to meet his own. "What's your real job?"

Tears stood in the blue eyes from the pain in his scalp, but James said, "I'm just a companion. An errand boy."

"Who's the girl?"

"She's my wife."

Warne stepped back, and Gordon shrugged the coat back upon his shoulders, bent down and retrieved the hat. Warne knew that outside of beating the younger man to a bloody pulp, he wouldn't get anything more out of him. James got up out of the chair and limped over to the door and turned there. "Next time," he promised, his eyes full of cruel anticipation. Next time he'd be on guard against the Judo business and Warne could look forward to some hurts. Say, something like a broken face and some cracked ribs and maybe a couple of fractured wrists.

"Shut the door as you go out," Warne snapped.

When Warne was alone again he sat there thinking about Gordon, and Gordon's errand boy, and Bellew. Bellew was next door now, winding up his affairs so he could close the office. He'd given Sandra a month's pay instead of notice and set her to work contacting the girls so they could look around for new representation.

Bellew seemed to have lost all interest in old man Gordon, or apparently in anything except peace and quiet and escape. He was cancelling the leases on the office and on his apartment, arranging to sell his furniture. Next, Warne thought, Bellew would take off on an aimless search for forgetfulness.

If it kept on, Bellew would end up as a bum, the anonymous letter writer would be vindicated, and Candy Carroll would go down as a suicide.

The prospect didn't please him.

I'd better meddle with it, Warne told himself.

There's nothing much I can do in the official investigation of Candy's death, whatever it was. So I'd better work on the Gordons. I won't be interfering with the cops, or running into newspaper men. I'll be covering all new territory. He corrected himself: old territory.

CHAPTER TEN

He telephoned the public stenographer downstairs. She had
worked before for him on matters involving the checking of
public records. He told her he wanted information about the date
of a death, surviving relatives and so forth, gave her Janie
Gordon's name and the approximate year. Then he asked that she
check old city directories of the same time for the address of a
Josiah Gray Gordon. If the L.A. public library couldn't help her
over the phone, she was to take a taxi down to the main library
and charge it to his account. He wanted the information fast.

Since he had requested just such items previously, she accepted
the job as a matter of routine.

Warne then went to Bellew's office. The inner door was shut and
he could hear Bellew's voice in there. Sandra was in the outer
room, clearing her desk. She looked up as Warne came in. "He's
in the other room using the phone."

"I came to see you," Warne said. "It occurred to me that you won't
be here next week, when I intended to ask for a second date.
Remember? What about tonight? We could take Dotty with us
and go out to eat, some quiet place, not a night club. And then I'll
take you both home."

She had paused with some papers in her hands. She looked at
him now in a mixture of perplexity and apprehension. But then
she said slowly, "I'd like to go. And it's nice of you to want Dotty,
too. I guess I'd better admit it: Dotty's kind of spoiled. You might
find her a ... a sort of brat." Her warm eyes searched his as if for
understanding. "You see, Aunt Faye never had any children of her
own. And she worships Dotty. She gives in to her every whim. And
I'm afraid Dotty takes advantage."

Warne smiled ruefully. "Well, it shows how wrong I can be. I'd
have figured Aunt Faye for a regular dragon, as far as kids were
concerned. All sorts of rules and regulations, don't do this and
don't do that. Watch your feet. That sort of thing. In fact, I had her

pegged for an old maid. She's a widow, then?"

Sandra nodded. "She and Uncle Monty had a long, happy marriage. She wasn't at all the way she is now; she wasn't harsh and opinionated, suspicious of everyone. They shared everything—making a living, the housework, the gardening. They owned a little stationery store in downtown L.A., in the financial district. Never made a lot of money. I guess Uncle Monty didn't have much business know-how. He never made any attempt to expand, or to increase the business. And some salesman was always palming something off on him that didn't sell well. But still, they had so much companionship and affection." Sandra shoved some papers into a folder. "Perhaps that's why she seems so anxious and embittered now."

"You aren't afraid the attitude might rub off on Dotty?"

"Oh, no. She spoils Dotty, that's all."

"Well, now that you've briefed me on what a juvenile fiend Dotty is, and I'm all braced for her—what about dinner?"

Her glance was amused and somewhat grateful. "Yes. I'd be happy."

Warne thought, somewhat to his own surprise: I guess it creeps up on you. My God, I'm falling for her! And here she was behind those horn rims and the business outfit, all these months!

He went on in to talk to Bellew. He told Bellew about the visit from James Gordon. "They're scared," he told Bellew. "They've got something to hide. Hell, I knew it the minute I saw the set-up. All the signs of money, the watchdog on the door."

Bellew seemed a shell of himself, an automaton moving in the memory of other times. "I don't care," he told Warne. "I'm not interested. Leave it alone."

"How can I, with Native Boy on my neck?"

Bellew said, "Whatever's with them—money or the lack of it, or a dozen big boys keeping everybody away from old man Gordon— it didn't have anything to do with Candy's death."

Warne leaned towards him across the desk. "You said yourself, this morning, 'He made it happen.'"

"I was thinking of the letters, that's all," Bellew said vaguely, with pain growing deep inside his haunted eyes. "And then, I was wrong. I wasn't thinking straight. Candy's death has no connection with Janie Gordon's suicide. Leave it all alone, Warne." He seemed almost pleading.

"You're afraid," Warne said. "I know exactly how you feel. You think if enough poking and probing goes on, it will land right back in your lap, the way Janie's suicide did."

Bellew fiddled with a stack of papers on his desk.

"Don't you see," Warne insisted, "that your only chance is to fight?"

Useless. He knew it. Bellew had no fight left in him. Specters thronged his thoughts, and far away in a corner of his own mind Bellew crouched, frozen with terror.

Fred Robinson slipped a bill to the man just inside the door. "I'd like to talk to Miss Anderson before she goes on. Where's the door, boy?"

The man inspected the bill. He was a tall distinguished figure in formal evening dress. Behind him lay the big room full of tables, softly lit, warmed by the muted gypsy music from the stage at the other end of the room.

The man indicated an obscure screen near the stage. "Behind that. Second door down the hall. Don't go barging in. You might see something would shock you."

"Shock a newspaper man?" Robinson echoed. "What on earth could it be?"

"Damned if I know, come to think of it," said the man tightly, turning to a party of four who had crowded up behind the reporter. Robinson threaded his way through the dining area to the screen; passed behind it to a narrow open doorway which led into a brightly lit hall. He rapped on the second door, listened to the rustle within, then opened it and peered inside. Chickie Anderson stood near the door in a costume made mostly of ostrich feathers; an older woman knelt beside her, plying a needle and thread on Chickie's bottom, and behind these two a dozen-odd girls sat at brightly mirrored tables applying makeup. Most of them wore kimonos. One of them looked at Robinson's intruding head and said, "Scat, cat. This is private property."

The woman in the black dress, sewing an ostrich feather on Chickie's bottom, looked at him fiercely and snapped, "Out. Before I call a cop."

"Can't you babies smell publicity when it's on your doorstep?" Robinson complained, letting his camera dangle into view. All eyes in the room instantly riveted themselves to this piece of apparatus. The wardrobe woman said uncertainly, "Who sent you?"

"I don't need anyone to send me," Robinson said impudently. "I'm a newspaper hack with my own byline. I take nice big glossy pics and they get printed in the public press. Need I say more?"

The woman looked behind her apprehensively, then leaped to her feet. There was a general outcry and a stampede, a shedding of kimonos which sailed through the air like a flock of kites. The wardrobe woman was caught in the melee, buffeted about, screamed at. Hoarse demands were made for emergency repairs. A flurry of ostrich plumes in all colors of the rainbow filled the room. Robinson grabbed Chickie's nerveless hand and yanked her through the door and closed it.

"Hi. Remember me?"

"Yes, I do. You're the reporter who was there with the policemen."

Robinson said, "Is there any little private room nearby where we can talk?"

"Nothing but the toilet. You wouldn't want to talk in there," Chickie answered primly.

"It's got a lock on the door, hasn't it?" He urged her away from the door, behind which the shrieks were rising in volume. "Where? Where?"

Looking somewhat embarrassed, Chickie led him into the ladies room.

"Good girl," Robinson commented, latching the door.

"I can't imagine why you want to talk to me again," Chickie said. "I've told everything I know. I've told it over and over again."

"There is some new evidence about Candy Carroll's death," Robinson said, trying to sound mysterious and important. "Some sounds heard by the other tenants. We think Candy must have had a visitor during the early part of the morning. Now think back. Are you sure Candy was asleep when you made that brief visit to pick up your swim suit?"

"I'd have sworn she was," Chickie said. "She didn't move or anything."

"Now, as you entered and left the building—did you notice anyone hanging around? A stranger? A strange woman, for instance?"

Chickie seemed uncertain. "It's an apartment house. A big one. I usually meet people in the hall. Somewhere."

"In the elevator, for instance?"

"I took the elevator up," Chickie said. "But I didn't wait for it, going down. I just trotted down the stairs, carrying my suit. You see, my friend gets a little impatient if I fool around."

Robinson seemed to be wrestling with some point of the story. "You got out of your friend's car, walked to the building, went indoors, rang for the automatic elevator."

"It was there already. Standing open in the lobby," Chickie supplied. "But I told the cops this. All of it."

"You went up in the elevator. Alone."

"I sure did," Chickie said agreeably.

"You noticed someone in the hall as you stepped out?"

A moment's surprise lit her face. "No, not then. Say, I'd forgotten about it!"

Robinson pounced. "When?"

"Well ... well, it must have been when I came out again with my swim suit. A very ... what you newspaper men would say, *fugitive* impression. It was like seeing a shadow, sort of. Am I confusing you?" When Robinson shook his head wryly, she hurried on, "Someone was down there just stepping out of another apartment. Just as I ducked into the stairway there was this movement, a door opening and someone coming out. Another tenant.'"

"A shadowy movement," Robinson summed up.

"Sort of."

"And then you rushed ... ran, you said—down the stairs."

"So my friend wouldn't be sore at me," Chickie reminded.

"Did you happen to hear any sounds, say for example a kind of insane laughter, as you ran from that floor?"

"Gosh, they don't let you have television on after ten o'clock," she told him. "After ten o'clock that's a very quiet building."

"This wasn't a TV program," he said. "It was either your friend Candy or some woman who was in there with her."

She sat looking up at him blankly. "I just don't dig it."

"Another tenant heard a woman's laughter. Maniacal. Hysterical."

"In my place?" Chickie cried, alarmed.

"Yes, in your place. Shortly after you'd gone. Surely you noticed someone slipping around, waiting to get into the apartment. This shadowy figure you glimpsed as you fled down those stairs—"

Chickie had begun to look worried. "Oh, that was just another tenant, Mr. ... uh ..."

"Robinson."

"Mr. Robinson. And as for my trip downstairs, well, I've told you, my friend down there in the car—"

"When you reached the lobby," Robinson said quickly, "what did you see?"

"See? Why, I saw those chairs and the desk, and that potted palm the manager's always fooling with. My God, it was all lit up. And nobody was down there laughing, either. It was quiet as a tomb."

"As a tomb," said Robinson, his bright eyes fixed on Chickie as if she were transparent and he could see through her to the headlines he was printing in his head.

Someone rattled the knob of the toilet door, and then there was a concerted screeching out in the hall. The girls had found him.

Robinson unlocked the door and went out, and was smothered in feathers and perfume and a dozen yammering voices. "Okay, girls. Okay. Look, I don't want this sort of crap, all of you made up and in your costumes. If I wanted anything like that I could get it off the press agent. I want something with human interest in it. I want you back in front of those mirrors using your lipsticks, doing your eyebrows and powdering your noses. And wearing those kimonos."

There was a concerted shriek as they turned from him and fought their way back towards the dressing room.

When they were back inside, screaming at each other to hurry, Robinson knelt quickly on the floor of the hall, yanked open the camera case, fitted a flash bulb and a plate, and said to Chickie, "Suck in your stomach and stick out your chest. Drop your left knee a little. No, move away from the toilet door. There's a sign on it."

Chickie stepped a few feet over, moving slowly and delicately as if bewildered by all the ruckus. "What will I do with my hands?"

Robinson had an inspiration. "Put your arms down at your sides. Stiff. And spread your fingers." He looked into the view finder. "Widen your eyes and quit grinning."

He caught her then on film—a lovely big-breasted girl pinned down by fright, back against the wall, her spread hands indicative of shock and alarm, her wide eyes searching as if for the flitting shadow she had glimpsed in the hall. Robinson thought: My God, it's perfect!

He took two more snaps, and then, since the noise in the dressing room had quieted a little and he judged the others would be expecting his appearance, he made a quiet and hasty departure.

CHAPTER ELEVEN

Warne picked up his phone. The public steno was on the line. "The Gordon death notice supplied an address. It's over twenty years old, of course. Used to be an old, run-down part of town, out near Bunker Hill."

"Fine. Shoot." Warne jotted down what she told him.

She added, "I'm going downtown to the main Public Library now, to look through old City Directories. It's on the way home, I won't charge you for the trip, just for the time I spend in there reading."

"You're a swell kid. I'm going to knock off here pretty soon, so don't bother to try to call back. I'll be here early tomorrow." They said goodbye and Warne hung up. He pushed the stuff on his desk into a couple of heaps, slammed the drawers on a file cabinet, took his hat out of the coat closet and went out. It was still early; he had plenty of time before he was to meet Sandra at Aunt Faye's.

He followed Sunset Boulevard all the way in to the old Plaza and then worked south. Well, the Gordon address at the time of Janie's suicide had certainly been in a shabby location, on the fringes of Chinatown; but during these last few years great changes had been made. Blocks of slums had been cleared, a vast new Civic Center had risen, and great channels had been gouged in the earth to accommodate the growing maze of freeways. It was gone. Nothing remained but white stone masonry and a tunnel roaring with traffic.

Working his way west again in the jet-propelled traffic of the Hollywood Freeway, Warne was busy piecing together his memories of years ago. He couldn't place the exact block where Janie must have lived—he'd only been a kid of ten or so, himself—but his dad had been fond of taking him and his mother to see the sights and to eat in old Chinatown, and the area in which the Gordons had lived, on its fringes, had been shabby, smelling, almost falling down. A mixture of races, too: Chinese, Mexican, a few Negroes and whites. Bellew said that the Gordons had come out from the middle west with the idea of promoting a dancing career for their daughter. Well, Warne thought, they must have arrived in a near-broke condition.

Perhaps the primary idea behind the move hadn't been so much a chance for Janie as the failure of the old man on his farm. Gordon had been getting up in years, must have been worn by toil, perhaps exhausted and simply looking for a place to lie down.

Warne tried to connect this thought with the image of the old man in the big luxurious home up the coast, and found that it didn't jibe. In spite of his extreme old age, Gordon was lively and malicious and alert. He had never, Warne decided, been the type of man to fade, to resign himself, in the face of difficulty. There was too much avaricious energy in him. He'd have found a way out.

Thinking of old man Gordon, Warne almost missed the turnoff near Western Avenue which would lead him to Aunt Faye's place.

When he located it, it proved to be a neat little frame house, painted white, with a small neat yard in which Warne saw a swing and teeter-totter, obviously put in for Dotty's benefit.

Sandra Shafer and the little girl were waiting in a porch swing. The house appeared closed and there was no sign of Aunt Faye. Warne parked his car and stepped out. Sandra and Dotty were off the porch now, hurrying his way. He thought that Sandra had almost an air of relief, of escape. He wondered briefly if there might have been a quarrel with the aunt.

Dotty had a pixie face, topped by black curls. She wore a white cotton pinafore, a pink jacket. She looked at Warne while Sandra introduced them to each other, and then said frankly, "Hello, Mr. Warne. My, but that's a funny necktie!"

Sandra was put out with her child. "Dotty, you know that wasn't a nice thing to say!"

"No," Warne put in, "Dotty's right. My taste in ties is complicated by the fact I'm somewhat color blind. I pick out something that appeals to me and it turns out I've got a dog. Most people put it much more impolitely than Dotty did." He shook hands with the young miss, who crinkled her eyes at him.

She had a rolled sheaf of papers, all colors and sizes. "Do you want to see my paintings?"

He took time to inspect the colorful blobs, noting meanwhile that Sandra was looking back apprehensively at the house.

They got into the car, Dotty between Warne and Sandra, and as they pulled away Sandra's sigh of relief was audible. Warne said, "Tired out from clearing up all of Bellew's tag ends?"

"Oh, no. As I said before, most of his business is in his hat. I didn't have a lot to do." She hesitated and then added frankly, "It's Aunt Faye. We had a ... a sort of spat."

"Not because of my calling for you, I hope."

She had taken off the glasses, loosened the slicked-back bun; her profile had a calm beauty that Warne liked. "No, not at all. This was over something else entirely." Again there was a thoughtful sort of quiet. "I wish Aunt Faye had kept her little shop after Uncle Monty died. She needs something to do. She needs to get out, to have contacts with other people. I didn't realize until just ... just today, how narrow and suspicious the poor old lady has become."

Dotty looked up into Warne's face. "Aunt Faye cried."

"I was tactless," Sandra hastened to say. She didn't add what she had been tactless about, and Warne was left with his curiosity unsatisfied. They ate in a quiet cafe and he took Sandra and Dotty home. He waited while Sandra ran a tub of water for the little girl, bathed her and put her to bed. Then they had an hour of quiet, friendly conversation. When Warne rose to go, she came at once into his arms to kiss him goodbye. Her lips were soft, pulsing with warmth. Her body folded itself against him, inside his arms, without prudery or hesitation. Warne knew all at once that Sandra Shafer had had a good marriage. She was the kind of woman who gave freely and warmly of herself. There was no meanness, no littleness in her.

He wondered how soon he could get her to marry him.

In the morning, the public steno called early with a list of old addresses. The Gordons had made a quick succession of moves, apparently, soon after their daughter's death.

Carrying the memo slip, Warne went next door; but no one was in Bellew's office today, apparently. He knew what Bellew would say, anyhow; Bellew no longer wanted any part of the Gordon family. Bellew was like an ostrich with its head in the sand.

Warne went out to his car, then reversed himself and walked around the corner for a newspaper. Fred Robinson's by-lined article about the mad laughter and about Chickie's shadowy intruder was on the front page, and Warne read it and frowned over it. In her feather costume, backed against a wall, hands spread as if to support herself, Chickie looked scared to death. This would certainly revive any flagging police interest, and they might easily take a second and closer look at Bellew. There must be a record somewhere, no matter how well buried, of Bellew's connection with the Gordon suicide. Once it was dug up and hit the papers, nothing on earth could save Bellew from a public pillorying. It stacked up amazingly. Two girls. Two jobs. Two deaths. And one miserable agent. Then Warne thought of the anonymous letter writer who had made Bellew's life wretched, and wondered in astonishment why there hadn't been a tip from that direction.

Surely the persecution of Bellew wouldn't be complete, from the letter writer's viewpoint, until the connection between the two cases was made public. As public as possible.

Why hadn't the tip come?

He puzzled over it all the way to the first of the addresses the steno had found for him.

This second home of the Gordons was in the Griffith Park district. He found the house without any trouble. It sat in the middle of the. block, among other homes of about the same size, a white bungalow with cocoa brown trim, the yard neat and well-kept. Warne drove past slowly; then parked and walked back. The house reminded him of Aunt Faye's in a way; it was about the same type and size. He decided that twenty-odd years ago the neighborhood had been pretty good. It was still old and respectable. The Gordons had taken a huge step up out of that slum, when their daughter had died. Warne recalled that Bellew had sold his business, given them the money—that could account for the improvement in surroundings.

He rang the bell and an elderly man answered the door. He told Warne that he and his wife were relative newcomers in the district, having bought the house on his retirement a little over two years ago. But yes, there were other people in the district who had lived here for many years. Three doors down to the left—try them. The Allens.

The Allens were at home. They were both very old. Mr. Allen wore a hearing aid and kept his mouth half-opened in a tense expression of wishing to catch everything. Mrs. Allen was shorter and rounder than her husband, wore a green gingham coverall apron, kept her hands in its pockets, and smelled as if she'd just finished baking a batch of cookies. They asked Warne in, listened to him, set about trying to recall the Gordons.

"She kept canaries," Mr. Allen decided in his high-pitched deaf man's voice.

"That was old lady Crooks," his wife corrected.

"He made lamps, then."

"No, he didn't. He's the one with inventions. The electrical inventions. I'm getting them, now. Long time ago, though," she added to Warne. "A real long time. And they didn't stay long. Poor Mrs. Gordon!"

"Why do you say that?" Warne asked interestedly.

"That poor woman didn't seem to know what was going on," Mrs. Allen told him. "She worried all the time and she seemed sort of lost. I don't think she understood what her husband was doing with his electrical business."

"He had an appliance store or something?"

"He invented things. In the garage. Not that I ever saw any of it. We were all as much in the dark as Mrs. Gordon was. It just looked like a big clutter and second-hand mess to me, but he was always telling us the money he was making with it. They got so rich they just moved away."

"What sort of woman was Mrs. Gordon?" Warne asked, thinking of Bellew's description of Janie's mother.

"Plain as a cow," said Mrs. Allen promptly. She told Warne, "I never saw her once in anything but a cotton house-dress. Old ones at that. He must have made a lot of money, but she didn't know anything about spending it. She moped a lot."

"Did she ever say anything about a recent death in the family?"

Mrs. Allen nodded. "She started to, once. She started to tell me about a daughter they had. But Mr. Gordon came in about that time and raised ned with her for talking about it. Said she didn't have good sense, the grief was over now, it was time to look at the future. Oh, he was a hard, quick kind of man. Mean, too, I used to think. He could have bought her a dress if he'd had to order it by catalogue." There was nothing more he could learn from the Allens, so Warne thanked them and left.

"Papa, I told you—"

The home in the Wilshire district was much larger and more impressive. The whole district exuded an air of settled prosperity and haughty aloofness.

Warne didn't stop. It was unlikely he would find here any approachable and garrulous old-timers like the Allens. These people had maids to answer their doors and before you saw any of them there would be a definite stating of business and purpose.

He had proof, though, of what he had only suspected: the wealth that made it possible for old man Gordon to live in his present style had had its beginnings in the few years immediately following his daughter's death. His financial rise had been almost meteoric. That garage with its clutter of second-hand electrical junk must have had all the possibilities of Aladdin's genie.

Or, of course, there was another and more likely explanation. Warne was inclined to it.

He tried to call Bellew at home, from a pay telephone, but no one answered the phone's ringing, nor did calling the office produce any better result.

At about noon, when Warne was back in his own office, Sandra telephoned. "Hello, Ed? I've just remembered where I saw that man. The one who passed in the street in a convertible."

"His name's James Gordon," Warne supplied.

"That isn't the name he gave me," she went on. "This happened longer-ago than I'd thought at first—oh, perhaps a year. It was about the time I went to work for Mr. Bellew. This man came into the office and asked about Mr. Bellew's agency, whether we might be interested in representing a young actor trying to get a foothold in Hollywood. He didn't exactly say he was the young actor in need of an agent, but I assumed it. Now I wonder, thinking back, if he wasn't just fishing for information."

"You mean—in the light of Bellew getting these poison pen letters?"

He thought she hesitated then; and was curious over it. "Well, no," she said finally. "I hadn't connected it with the letters."

Warne thought, if old man Gordon had wanted to find out whether Bellew was still in the business of sending girls out on party dates, it was just the sort of maneuver he'd plan.

Had it marked the beginning of a plot which had culminated in Candy Carroll's death?

CHAPTER TWELVE

At the newspaper offices, all gripes from readers were transferred to a character named Wetz, a proof man in a dark little cubbyhole on the rear of the third floor. At about twelve-thirty on the day of Robinson's second article about Candy's death, a woman with an excited, loud, nasal voice demanded of the switchboard girl to be connected with Robinson at once. The girl, scenting a beef, promptly switched the call to Wetz.

Wetz was correcting the previous day's race chart, a mean, close, demanding job. He heard the woman shout: "Are you the man who wrote this article in the paper about Miss Anderson?"

Wetz grunted, his customary response during these opening moments.

"If you are, Mr. Robinson—and of course I know you are—I want to explain just how wrong your whole story is from beginning to end. Why, it didn't happen at all the way you said! You see, I live on that same floor, the same one with Miss Anderson's apartment, just down the hall a way, and *I* was the person she sort of glimpsed stepping out of a door as she hurried into the stair well."

"Hmmmmmm," said Wetz. "Hmmmm. You were saying?"

"I saw her distinctly. Of course I wasn't looking back quickly over my shoulder, as she was. I had a direct view. I saw that she had something bright, a small gay-colored garment like a swim-suit, in one hand. And that she seemed to be in a terrible hurry. But as for calling me an ominous shadow—it's nonsense!"

"I see," said Wetz wearily into the phone.

"I resent the implication that I am a dangerous, lurking sort of person," the woman said, louder than ever. "Even if people don't connect this ridiculous story with me—Eva Macklin!"

"We'll see what we can do, ma'am."

"I won't be satisfied with anything less than a complete retraction and apology. I can't have people thinking of me as a— a fiend!"

"We'll take care of it."

She subsided a little. "Besides, such misconstruction of the facts might impede the official investigation of Miss Carroll's death."

"Don't worry about it," he muttered; marking hieroglyphics on the proofs.

"Well ... thank you for being so co-operative," she concluded briskly.

Wetz murmured something soothing and hung up. He found a piece of scratch paper and scribbled: *You goofed about some woman in a hall*, and called a boy and told him to put the paper on Robinson's desk.

Robinson never saw the paper. When he came in later that day he took up the collection of odds and ends and dumped them into a basket. He had a new line on the story now, and was quite excited over it. The police were beginning to consider seriously a theory that Candy Carroll might have been pushed out of that window after all.

There had been splinters under Candy's nails, off the frame of the broken screen, proving that on her way out she'd scratched like a cat for a toehold.

Furthermore, there had been wool fibres clenched between Candy's teeth. Robinson was sure that Candy wouldn't have gone in for woolen toothbrushes. It looked as if she might have bitten someone—say, through a coat.

Robinson's pipeline into the police department was solid and discreet. He set happily to work, clackety-clack on the machine, bolder now about calling it murder; and when a copy boy rushed past the desk, the scrap of paper with Wetz's memo drifted to the floor and was lost.

Robinson wouldn't have paid any attention to it, anyway.

Chickie slept until nearly three, making up for the broken slumber of the previous day. When she wakened, she rolled over in bed, glanced at the little gilt clock, then sat up and stretched. Chickie got out of bed, impelled by she knew not what, and twitched the cords on the venetian blinds to let in the day. Her legs were white, smooth and shapely below the short hem of the abbreviated gown.

She padded out across the living room and opened the door. Her paper lay propped against the lintel. She brought it in and stood in the middle of the floor to read the latest developments in the investigation of Candy's suicide. Her picture pleased her. It had a lot of drama, showed that she knew how to express emotion. Someone important ought to notice it, she thought. Someone like Metro-Goldwyn-Mayer, for instance. The wide eyes, the pose as if backed to a wall seemed to Chickie the epitome of dramatized fright.

She took the paper with her when she returned to the kitchen. She filled a glass with orange juice, made toast, poured herself coffee and sat down to eat with the paper propped in front of her. The little kitchen was filled with afternoon sunlight, cheerful and clean, and as soon as she had eaten and had gotten fully awake, Chickie felt wonderful. Why, she was a celebrity!

In ecstasy, she raised her arms over her head, stretching herself inside the short, filmy gown, lifting her face in a dazzling smile to the ceiling. She felt as if the eyes of the whole world were on her at this instant, admiring, envying, idolizing. The dream was interrupted by the ringing of the doorbell.

She padded back through the living room to the door. It was Mrs. Macklin who lived down the hall. The tall sallow woman seemed excited over something. Chickie was still so wrapped up in her sudden fame that it took a minute or so before she got the drift of Mrs. Macklin's conversation.

"I saw that your paper had been taken in, so I knew you must be awake and up," Mrs. Macklin said. "I wanted you to know that I've already set forces in motion to retract that awful story. If there's no retraction I intend to sue that dreadful man."

"What dreadful man is that?" Chickie wondered.

"That Robinson creature." Mrs. Macklin failed to notice the startled look which came over Chickie. She was, however, staring at Chickie's gown. "He wrote the story. His name's right there on it, beside that picture of you. Why, I never heard such nonsense!"

It occurred to Chickie that this woman represented trouble and something had to be done about her. "Won't you come in?"

"I've only a moment. I'm on my way to shop." Mrs. Macklin stepped in over the sill and Chickie shut the door behind her. "No, I won't bother to sit down. I just wanted you to know that I had already acted in our behalf. I'll buy a paper later on and if there isn't a suitable explanation, I'll contact the editor himself."

"You called Mr. Robinson?" Chickie surmised.

"I certainly did. I told him that *I* was the person who stepped out into the hall as you started down those stairs."

"You were?" Chickie cried, aghast. Why, this woman was blowing the nice story completely apart! She was going to ruin everything! "I … uh … I must have confused Mr. Robinson, then," Chickie said, her mind working at forced-draft. "You see, it was … it was on another floor I noticed this … uh … prowler."

"There was a prowler?" Mrs. Macklin yelped. "Here? In this building?"

"Well, someone got in here and made Candy laugh," Chickie said, more in the way of self-vindication than with any delusion she'd really seen anyone. There had been a visitor, hadn't there? she told herself. Candy wasn't the kind of girl who went batty and laughed like a hyena while she was all alone trying to sleep.

"What do you mean?" Mrs. Macklin demanded. "Made her laugh?"

Chickie said, "Didn't you know? Well, you're down at the corner of the building. Probably it didn't wake you. It was perfectly awful. Like a—a maniac."

Mrs. Macklin now began to study Chickie uneasily. "You should have told someone instead of rushing off like that."

"Oh, I didn't hear the laughter. The woman downstairs did. At three o'clock, long after I'd gone to the swimming party. Didn't you read Mr. Robinson's article all the way through?"

"I skipped," Mrs. Macklin admitted. "Why, then," she exclaimed suddenly, "it might mean that Miss Carroll didn't commit suicide!"

"I guess it might," Chickie admitted uneasily.

"She was murdered!" A spot of color burned in each of Mrs. Macklin's sallow cheeks.

Chickie hadn't expressed it to herself as yet in such definite terms. Now, with Mrs. Macklin coming out flatly with such a statement, Chickie found her ground shifting. All at once she had a queer feeling that it might be better not to be directly involved in a murder case.

Mrs. Macklin had gone back to the doorway. "Well, I'd better be running along. I won't call the newspaper again. I'd just be making a fool of myself."

"Oh, it's best to keep the record straight. I'm glad you called," Chickie said vaguely. She glanced behind her, then. The phone was ringing.

"Hello?" Chickie said.

"Mr. Spencer asked me to call," said a slightly hoarse voice in her ear, "and find out if you could come in a half-hour early tonight?"

"A half-hour early? Why ... why, sure."

Chickie waited, expecting the caller to explain. "Is there going to be a change in the show, or something?"

"Probably," said the caller in a sort of enigmatic tone, and the line clicked as the other phone was replaced.

Well, if the manager, Mr. Spencer, wanted her there a half-hour early, she'd be there right on the button.

Funny, though, he'd had someone call her for him. Usually he had plenty of time during the afternoon, he arranged any program changes himself.

The voice on the phone had been totally unfamiliar. Chickie tried to place it, running over various employees of the club to herself, but failed.

She switched on the radio for some music and settled down to do exercises in time to it. Chickie was watchful of her measurements. She was just right now, a lovely 39-24-36; and she meant to stay that way. Any minute, she might be noticed by someone from Fox or Metro.

Warne was about done for the day. He had a couple of calls to make on his way home, and he was through. The phone rang and when he picked it up, Sandra said, "I just got home, Ed. Were you able to get hold of Mr. Bellew?"

"Yes, I finally did. I'm going out there pretty soon. He's got to buck up and face this thing out. If he caves in, he's a dead duck. Everything he has will go down the drain."

"Will you tell him about this James Gordon coming in to see me about a year ago?"

"I sure will."

"Why don't you come to my house for dinner—say, tomorrow night? I'll have steak. Any way you want it."

"Could it be," Warne wondered, "that you're beginning to have designs on me?" He was hoping her answer might give him a clue to her real feelings but she merely said lightly: "Never. And spoil that lovely freedom of yours?"

"I thought when women started to cook—"

"They're feeling charitable, that's all."

"I'm not pinning you down a bit," he complained.

"Not a bit," she agreed. "Goodbye, Ed. Tell Mr. Bellew about that James Gordon for me."

He locked up the office, made the two required business calls to settle some insurance angles, then took Sunset Boulevard west, towards Beverly Hills. He had to see Bellew. He wanted Bellew to keep that office open, keep Sandra there. Even part time—it gave him a chance to see her. He had an unpleasant feeling he might lose her, otherwise.

CHAPTER THIRTEEN

As one excuse for coming, Warne had brought the pictures Aunt Faye had stripped off the walls. He carried them wrapped in a sheet of newspaper, and as he entered Bellew's modern oriental living room, Bellew gave the package a nervous glance and said, "What's that?"

"Your art gallery." Warne dropped the package on a low white table. "I'd keep them for pornographic purposes, but I have ambitions to become a decent married man. Never leave anything where it might be snatched up by a newspaper man. Incidentally—" Warne had spread the newspaper wrapping. "—this particular picture of Miss Carroll looks as if it might have come out of your collection. It's been retouched, of course. Robinson was in your office, alone. I'll bet he swiped it before I rushed in there."

Bellew sank down on the couch. His eyes had fastened themselves on the sheet of newsprint. "What do you think of Miss Anderson's story?"

"I think she's a sap."

Bellew glanced at him inquiringly.

"I think she let Robinson spin a yarn and put it into her mouth," Warne added. "It made a better story. I'd like to know what the truth sounded like."

Bellew rubbed his hands together. "I've been expecting something else to break. You know what I mean."

"The link to Janie Gordon? Yes, I don't understand it. The opportunity seems too good to miss. All the letters prophesying what would happen, and then it does happen—and now, nothing." Warne sat down in a white leather chair with tapering black legs, accepted a cigarette and a light from Bellew. "If I were you, I'd take heart from it."

Bellew shook his head dismally. "It doesn't mean anything."

"Well of course, it has to mean *something*," Warne said, half-angry at Bellew's impenetrable mood.

"The first possibility is that this letter writer had something to do with the Carroll girl's death. Now he's frightened at the lengths he has gone, the madness or whatever it was, abnormal hatred perhaps, which drove him to kill the girl simply to complete the pattern laid out in the letters. He's still got sense enough to lay low, not to write any more letters, hope that the cops never catch on to his ugly part in this."

Bellew lit a cigarette for himself. Warne noticed how his fingers shook.

"The second possibility, obviously, is that the person who wrote the letters had nothing at all to do with the death. Candy Carroll just happened to commit suicide. She jumped at the exact moment to shock hell out of your correspondent. He ... or she ... is stunned and even terrified that the thing prophesied in the letters has actually come to pass."

"Of course," Bellew said wearily, "I see these two opposing possibilities but seeing them doesn't give any answer."

"It might, in this way," Warne insisted. "If it turns out that Candy Carroll was killed, was pushed from that high window, it will be logical to assume that the letter writer committed the murder."

"And if ... if it was suicide?"

"Then, as I said, your letter writer is laying low from shock."

Bellew shoved the nude photos distractedly into a cabinet, then returned to his chair. "Do you have any hint as to who wrote those damned letters?"

"I've got a pretty good idea."

"Who is it?"

Warne shook his head. "I can't speak out on a mere suspicion."

"You could tell me. I'd treat it in strict confidence."

Warne changed the subject abruptly. "I want to tell you what I've found out in regard to the Gordons."

Bellew's tone was almost violent, "I don't want to hear about them!"

"Yes you do. You put old man Gordon on the track of a gold mine.

You sent him way up in the world."

"I want to talk about those letters," Bellew exploded. "What do I care what's happened to Gordon in the years since I caused his kid's death? To hell with it. You'd better remember this—that document expert said the letters were most likely to have been written by a woman. Now, is this person you're thinking about a woman? Is she?"

"One of two," Warne said. "But I don't know which one, and I'm not going to spout off on guesses."

Bellew seemed almost to sulk. The sideburns, frosted with gray on either side of his face, gave him a wary, foxy look.

"What would you do if I told you?" Warne asked curiously.

"I don't know. Something pretty ugly, I'm afraid."

"And yet—you insisted, before, that the letters had nothing to do with Candy's death. You almost convinced me."

"I know. And they didn't have—I'm sure. But whoever wrote those letters has a big account to settle." Suddenly an almost fanatical anger burned in the depths of Bellew's eyes. "I'll pay that score if I ever get the chance." He sat hunched over, wringing his hands.

"Well, don't you want to hear what I've learned about the Gordons?"

Bellew shrugged, not looking up. "Yeah. Sure. Go ahead."

"When you met the Gordons, you said they were a typical transplanted farm couple. No airs, no signs of money. You felt so sorry for them you gave them the money you realized from selling your agency."

Bellew made an impatient motion with his head.

"I can tell you something more. At the time their daughter died they were living in a slum. But almost at once after the girl was gone, their financial picture improved to a startling degree."

Bellew just looked blank.

"The second house they moved into wasn't paid for by the kind of money you'd given them. It's almost a mansion. Old man Gordon rigged up some electrical junk in his garage and said he was an inventor. I don't think anyone believed it. But he did obtain money, a lot of it, and his standard of living shot up in proportion. I think he got the dough out of one of those men who had raped his girl."

Bellew said bitterly, "Well, by God, do you blame him?"

Warne shrugged. "I can't help wondering if you've told everything about your dealing with Gordon, whether he didn't put the bite on you later on for more money."

"You can't get blood out of a turnip," Bellew said grimly.

"He's been checking up on you since, though," Warne told him. "I was in the street with Sandra when Native Boy drove by, and she's remembered now—this James Gordon came around almost a year ago, checking up on you."

Bellew kept his head lowered. Warne couldn't see whether the news interested or alarmed him.

"What I'm getting around to is this—if Gordon was interested in getting more money now, and if the letters came from someone at his house, they might have been an attempt to soften you up for another touch."

Bellew's eyes came up and his mouth tightened to a thin line. "You think so?"

"He's a damned mercenary old man," Warne said. "Not many men would have commercialized their daughter's suicide. And now that he's outlived the mortality tables and is getting ready to collect his life insurance—you should see him."

"You think he had someone write me those letters?" Bellew insisted.

"It's a possibility. I'd like your permission to investigate further into it."

"Hell, go ahead!" Bellew got up and walked tensely about, working his shoulders nervously inside his well-cut coat. "As long as you don't insist I tell the police about the letters—go ahead, find out all you can."

"I want you to open your office tomorrow as if nothing had happened," Warne added. "That's important."

Bellew flung around to face him. "I've closed the office! I'll never go there again."

"You will if you want this thing settled," Warne told him. "Don't you see that the office is the contact, the focal point? Keeping it open means you're inviting further feelers?"

"I can't take it any longer," Bellew said miserably, reverting to his air of defeat.

"Let Sandra come in for a week, anyhow."

Bellew seemed to think it over. "All right, then. If she's willing."

Warne said, "There might even be another letter."

The grimness returned to Bellew's eyes. "I'd like to catch someone delivering it!"

Chickie Anderson stood in panties and bra before the mirror, putting mascara on her lashes. She glanced occasionally at the clock, aware of the passing of time and of the fact that she was supposed to go a half-hour earlier to the club. She picked out a smartly styled gray silk dress, gray suede pumps, a short red jacket. When she was dressed she went to the mirror again for a final touch at her hair.

She turned slowly. "For a bag, you're pretty good." The gray silk was tight across her cone-shaped breasts and the little jacket lay open to reveal this. Chickie took a gray handbag out of the dresser drawer and stuffed into it a wallet, some change, makeup, cleansing tissues, and a small gold whistle. The whistle had been a gift from a manager she'd liked. He'd said, "Use it, kid, and I'll come running."

She had never used it to call that particular man, because he was so much older and married with a family and Chickie couldn't see any future to a friendship with him. Once in a while, on a lonely street at night, waiting for a bus after a late engagement, Chickie had found comfort in its possession. It made a shrill, piercing noise. Most of all, Chickie used it as a conversation piece and as a sort of good-luck charm.

She went out, locking the apartment door. Downstairs in the lobby Chickie ran into the woman manager, who told her that the police had come back for the broken window screen, and that a newspaper photographer had even taken its picture.

"They wouldn't tell me nothing," the woman complained, "but I got a hunch it means something. I think they were looking at it for fingernail scratches. Like maybe, your friend tried to claw her way back in, once she was half-outside."

Chickie thought of something. "Did anyone hear her scream?"

"Come to think of it, no. Or I guess not. Nobody mentioned it to me and I've heard every story going, including that crazy Mrs. Hackendyke's who says she heard somebody laughing."

Chickie put a thoughtful finger to her chin. "You know, I've been thinking about that. Mr. Robinson told me about it. And I thought, if it was Candy doing it, laughing at someone who was up there with her ... well, I sort of have an idea what kind of person would make her laugh."

"You do?"

"Yes, I sort of do," Chickie said hesitantly.

"A young feller, a boy friend, telling her a joke?"

"Oh, no," Chickie said. "This kind of laughing was hysterical. Almost insane, Mr. Robinson said. And you know, to a girl like Candy, not many things would seem that funny. I mean, with a boy friend for instance, Candy was sort of mysterious. She liked to keep men guessing. But one time, there was this little old lady at a bus stop, and we got to talking. Candy was there with me. This little old lady was a card! I mean, terribly proper. You just knew she'd never done anything ...uh ... oh, you know—naughty. Never at all. She had on high button shoes and cotton gloves. Really!"

"And Candy ... Miss Carroll ... thought the little old lady was funny?" the manager wondered.

"It was this experience—"

"Excuse me," the manager interrupted. "I see it's getting dark outside. I'd better turn on the lights."

Candy recalled with a start that time was passing, that she was due early at the club. She ran outside, hurried down the steep slope to the freeway, walked to the gate which admitted bus passengers to the area where the bus stopped. Waiting, her mind turned to that other time, months past now, when she and Candy had happened to wait where the little old lady had noticed them. It had been embarrassing at the end. Candy just hadn't been able to control her mirth and the little old lady had seemed sort of angry at them. She had been a very, very proper person; and after Candy had listened to her for a while she had simply burst with laughter.

"It makes you sort of think," Chickie murmured, staring out at the traffic rushing past on the freeway.

The Chatter Box Club was out near Culver City, at the end of a short street that rose into the fringes of the Baldwin Hills. The bus went west on Jefferson Boulevard, passing R.K.O. and M.G.M. studios; and Chickie got off near the big golf courses. It was a quiet district and somewhat off the beaten track. The Chatter Box capitalized on the privacy. It had been in the same spot for a long time and had a lot of old, steady customers.

Where she got off, on the boulevard, there was a small shopping center, a few stores and a theatre, all brightly lit; but between this and the club was a stretch of vacant sidewalk overhung with trees. When she alighted from the bus, Chickie glanced around. Sometimes there were others there, on their way to work, and she walked with them.

She was surprised not to find anyone she knew. Surely everyone had had an early call. She strolled along, a little baffled by it.

It seemed uncannily quiet and her steps echoed. Other sounds seemed to follow along like an uneasy breath stirring the trees. Chickie looked up the empty street towards the club at the end of the block, expecting the glow of neon; but the sign wasn't lit yet. There was only the big light on its standard in the parking lot. Through the trees it made a lacy pattern that covered her, flecked the gray dress and the red coat and twinkled between her feet. She had a sudden urge to hurry.

A voice came out of the dark, speaking her name, a summons. Chickie stopped and turned. Behind her the sidewalk stretched emptily, all the way down to the busy corner and the shopping area. Chickie shook her head. She must be hearing things.

The voice spoke again, and Chickie turned with a paralyzed slowness to stare into the unrelieved darkness between the trees. "Who is it?" She waited, her mouth going dry. "Mr. Spencer? Is it you, Mr. Spencer?" There was no answer. The small uneasy wind stirred the trees; Chickie felt its breath on her face. She fumbled with the catch on her purse. She had remembered the little gold whistle. Perhaps she needed it just now. There was something quite strange about this voice, the darkness, and the empty street.

She half-lifted the whistle to her lips, and waited, aware of the pulse pounding in her temples and the faint chill like the breath from an opening underground that ran along her skin.

She sensed, rather than saw or heard, the sizzling blow. She tried to duck. She tried to put the whistle between her lips. But then, there wasn't time for either. Something exploded against the side of her head and even as her senses dizzied she felt terrible hands ripping at her dress, she felt cold night air rush in upon her uncovered flesh, and then she was being dragged into the dark beneath the trees.

CHAPTER FOURTEEN

At first no one connected what had happened to Chickie Anderson with the fact that she was a witness in the Candy Carroll case. Chickie had been discovered on her hands and knees, dragging herself out of the shrubbery, by a customer walking up to the Chatter Box bar for a drink. She'd been wearing nylons and shoes, not a stitch else, and the first thing which occurred both to the police and to the newspapers was that here was another in the long series of rape and attack cases which had plagued L.A. She had been horribly abused, possibly left for dead by her assailant, but still she lived. She was rushed to a hospital where the doctors stifled her screams with sedatives. The nurses treated her wounds, washed dirt and leaves off her, and put her in a white cotton hospital gown. They lowered the lights and shut the door, leaving a nurse in there with her. She was unable to speak coherently about what had happened to her, perhaps never would.

It was Robinson who broke the complete story the next morning, along with new facts about Candy Carroll. The Carroll death was now definitely considered a murder and Robinson linked that fact up with the sneak attack on Chickie. He pointed out that someone had killed Candy Carroll and made it look like suicide, and now they'd tried to kill Chickie and make it look like a casual mugging and rape. The paper ran Chickie's picture again, the one where she stood wide-eyed and glued to the wall.

Warne picked up a paper as he went into his office. He had unlocked his door, hung up his hat, had laid the paper on the desk and was still standing and looking at it, when he heard someone come in behind him. He turned quickly. The girl was young, slim, and beautiful. She had a pert face, black hair cut in the style girls call a Dutch Bob—and she was James Gordon's wife. "Mr. Warne? Are you open for business?" she asked cutely.

"Now where have I heard that voice before," Warne mused.

"Let's see, were you ever on television?"

"Let's don't kid around, Mr. Warne." She came closer and he caught the perfume she wore. She was right out of a jungle. Green eyes, too. Eyes with a faintly reptilian fixity, as if she might be trying to mesmerize him as a snake fixes a bird. "I telephoned you, yes. Several days past. I wanted to do you a favor. Probably you don't believe that."

"It does, stretch my credulity a bit. Why the concern for me?"

She shrugged, made a small pursed mouth. "I don't like to see perfectly innocent bystanders get bruised. But I'm not here to talk about that. I'm here to say that I think my husband was most stupid and tactless day before yesterday. He shouldn't have done what he did."

"Does he feel that way?"

"He's so repentant," she said, pinning him with the green stare.

"Oh, I'll bet."

"No, he really is. And Uncle Gray is furious. You see, his uncle just wanted him to find out what you meant by coming to him under false pretenses and describing Bellew as you did."

Warne shook his head, looked into her pouting eyes. "Suppose I had simply asked if he knew Bellew. A direct question."

A slightly displeased expression settled in her face. "Oh, I think Uncle Gray would have denied knowing that awful little man. Just to be cagey. And knowing nothing about you." She put a big white purse on Warne's desk and let herself down into a chair. All of her movements were delicate and graceful. She wore a severely cut green sheath dress and it showed off the slim form, the small high breasts and flat hips which made her seem too young for the sophistication in her manner. "But now he has another idea."

"Let me guess," said Warne dryly, sitting on the edge of the desk.

"You don't have to. I'll tell you. He wants money. He's always thinking about money and now this unpleasantness has come up about some girl Bellew sent out, and Uncle Gray thinks Mr. Bellew might pay him to keep still about some other old affair."

"It really was Gordon, then, who sent Bellew those letters."

"You mentioned something about letters during our previous

conversation," she said, frowning. "I don't understand you."

"Let it go. Is Gordon willing to risk exposure as a blackmailer?"

She laughed. "It would be handled very carefully. I doubt if Bellew could prove anything afterwards." She stood up, came to the desk, opened the white purse and extracted cigarettes, put a cigarette between her lips and then waited for Warne to give her a light. As his hand holding the lighter came close, she seized his wrist and he felt the scratchly tickle of her long silver-tinted nails.

After she had the cigarette going, still standing near him, she asked: "You are still representing Bellew, aren't you?"

"Why? Have you tried to contact him direct?"

"I couldn't get him." She said it ruefully, then seemed to cheer up at some new idea. "Look, darling. I like you. And with you acting for Bellew and me for Uncle Gray, we could make things mutually profitable." She waited, watching narrowly. "You like me too, don't you?"

He put his hands on her flat hips and pulled her tight against him. The green eyes had the brightness of emeralds up close like this, and the jungle perfume made him think of hot nights by a steaming river. "You're a hell of a lot prettier than old man Gordon. But I want to see him. Talk to him. In person."

She pulled Warne's face down and kissed him with parted lips as if she were anxious to know if he would let her. Her mouth had an unexpected flavor, cool as mint. Something in the lipstick, Warne thought. He felt her tap his chin with a tinted nail. "I'll let you see him. He's just a silly old man. Money-mad. As for me … I've just got awfully, awfully sticky fingers."

"Let's go, then," Warne said, pushing her off. Her eyes flew wide.

There were a lot of mental reservations swimming in the green eyes, too. "Well … all right. We can go in my car."

He shook his head, sensing tricks. "I'll follow you up the coast."

She pushed herself against him, putting arms around his neck, kissing him again with the parted, mint-flavored mouth. Her tongue flicked in to touch his own. The green eyes were nearly shut, the color darkened under her lashes. Warne thought, James has got himself quite a woman. I wonder if he knows how hard she plays when he's not around. She's wearing herself out.

He was in his own car, his hand on the key in the switch, when he changed his mind. He hurried back into the building, upstairs, opened the office door and went across to his desk. In an upper drawer was a souvenir given him by a buddy in the Army. A big heavy ring, the color of cut steel. He slipped it on the middle finger of his right hand, looked at it and grinned slightly. Made in Germany. Made for some Nazi with a taste for cute knick-knacks. Warne had never felt the urge to wear it before. "I'm getting vain," he muttered to himself, re-locking the office door. "I've got to have something, after all, to match those silver fingernails."

The big ring gleamed in the light.

He didn't catch sight of her at all, all the way up the coast. The morning was bright and traffic wasn't too heavy. She must have flown the Cad like a jet, Warne told himself. At the big brick wall, topped with ivy, he slowed. It all looked finer, larger, more luxurious, now that he had those other places to compare with it, the houses Gordon had lived in on his way up.

He turned in at the wide gateway and drove the winding, flower-bordered street to Gordon's home. He parked the car and got out. The Cad was here already, at the other end of the driveway, its nose against the garage door. Warne went to the door and rang the bell. The place had an intense air of silence about it, Warne thought suddenly. He pushed the bell button again, and then the door opened and there was James Gordon as he had first seen him, native pants and all.

Well, not quite the same, Warne decided. You could see where Native Boy had rammed that office wall. The eyes were careful and remote, as if Warne might see something in them James wasn't ready to show. "Hello, Warne," said James Gordon. He stepped back a little. "Come in. Madge is in the back with my uncle."

The tone was controlled. Wayne walked past. He heard James shut the door and glanced back. James was shutting the door without looking at it. His eyes were on Warne's back, between the shoulder blades. About the spot, Warne thought, he might like to put a knife.

Warne said, "No hard feelings?"

"Uncle Gray doesn't like hard feelings," James said discreetly.

"Lead the way, then," said Warne.

James hesitated for only a moment. Then he stepped past Warne and went down the hall, as before, past the other rooms to the big enclosed place at the rear of the house. Warne looked past him. The black haired girl in the tight sheath stood beside Mr. Gordon's empty wheelchair. James looked over his shoulder. "Uncle Gray isn't here. Excuse me while I get him, will you?"

Warne went on out into the open sunny roofless room. The girl gave him a sultry glance, then smiled. "You didn't keep up with me," she said. "I meant to stop and look at the water for a while. There are several good spots along the beach."

"It's daytime, baby. That's for after dark."

A small smile quirked her vivid lips. She stepped across the paved area to its other side. At the same moment Warne saw James Gordon in the doorway to the hall. He had taken off his shirt. His upper torso, smooth as satin and as brown as oaken beams, gleamed with grease. He squatted a little, flexing his knees, and his arms went out, his hands spread in a wrestler's attitude.

He waddled forward into the sun. The light blazed in the white butch cut. There was sweat on his upper lip and along the bunched muscles of his biceps. "I feel highly overdressed," Warne complained.

"Anything you want, this time," James grunted. "Judo. The Works. You name it."

Warne made a deprecating gesture. "My God, I was just defending myself. You didn't have to take it personally."

"I liked taking it personally," James said. "I've had a bit of Judo myself. You just caught me off guard, that was all. I thought of hitting you with my fists because that's the natural and common way. But when anyone gets clever with me I like to get clever right back at them."

James was circling a little, while Warne seemed to back away in alarm.

"Hey, no fair! I've got all my clothes on!" Warne cried.

"Shut up and fight."

"Is this your uncle's idea?" Warne pleaded as if seeking a reprieve.

"Nothing to do with Uncle Gray." James made a feint and Warne put up his hands half-heartedly, just making a gesture, as if knowing he was already whipped. Warne kept his hands up as if behind them he might make a desperate break, perhaps run for the door or something equally foolish. There was a tiny, almost inaudible metallic click. The next instant James moved in on Warne like a greased brown flash.

Warne brushed at him with an awkward, broken motion. Warne's hand went across his face, then jerked slightly lower, changing direction, swept downwards almost as if he were doffing a hat. The back of his hand made contact with the smooth brown skin. James Gordon stumbled. He had been reaching for Warne's throat but now his fingers trembled up to touch his own face.

He turned, blanching with shock, and Madge Gordon stared with frozen green eyes. Then she screamed. A vast red mouth gaped across the middle of her husband's face. From throat to belt the front of his body lay opened as if a surgeon had slit it with a scalpel.

Warne looked at the ring on his right hand. From the center of the polished steel cabochon a tiny blade now protruded. It was red with blood, but through the blood it glittered with a terrible sharpness.

"The Germans always were clever," he said to Madge Gordon.

She didn't hear him. She was still screaming. Her husband had fallen to his knees.

CHAPTER FIFTEEN

James Gordon had rolled over on his back and was holding his face together between pinched finger-tips. He whispered hoarsely to his wife, "Get a doctor, for God's sake!"

She had stopped screaming. She seemed dazed and revolted, unable to grasp what had happened. She looked at Warne. "What shall I do?"

"What he said. Call a doctor. If you don't he's going to have some interesting scars."

She pounded her small fists together. "I ought to get the police."

"How much publicity can the old man take?" Warne asked. "A little? A lot? Is anyone looking for him? If you get the cops out here you'll all make the front pages. As for me, I don't give a damn."

She ran her fingers through the thick black hair. "Why did you cut him like that?"

"Why did you bring me here to be beaten up? So Native Boy could even up the score? How bad was it going to be? Something interesting like a broken leg or an arm? Or just a smashed face?"

"He said you needed a lesson."

"I learned that lesson years ago," said Warne with contempt. He walked away into the house. He turned left, found himself in an enormous kitchen fitted with a fireplace, an electric spit and indoor barbecue. He retraced his way and found the wing with the bedrooms. Mr. Gordon was in one of them, in a big four-poster bed under a white satin counterpane. He was propped up with pillows. In his ancient face the dark eyes were crazily alive. "What happened out there?" he demanded when Warne came in.

"Your orders. You should remember them. Your boy was just trying to carry them out."

A secret glee flickered through the wrinkled mask. "I didn't really want any rough stuff. I want peace and quiet and privacy."

"And money," Warne added. "Who's after you? One of those men you blackmailed twenty-odd years ago? Or an heir who went to the cupboard and found it empty?"

The old man smiled. "You're pretty clever. Bellew's a fool and as long as he was by himself, I didn't worry. I knew I had to stop you."

"Who's got you scared?" Warne persisted.

The old hands tightened on the satin spread. They were like hawk's claws, thin, talon-like. "Heirs. But they can't prove anything."

"You think that fiddling around with the electric junk in the garage was enough cover?"

A startled, attentive expression, came over Mr. Gordon. "Got onto that, huh?"

"Yes, and it's lousy."

"If they take it all away from me now there won't be a thing to leave to James and Madge." He cackled over if, and spittle settled on his chin. "Not a thing. And they'll be broke. And. Madge likes nice things."

"You can give them the insurance," Warne advised, and thought: he's planning to leave them nothing. He doesn't give a damn for them, and here they are, giving their young lives in his service. Degrading themselves. "What I'm interested in are the letters Bellew's been getting. Did you have Madge type them for you?"

"Madge doesn't type," the old man said promptly. "She does scarcely anything but paint her nails and brush her hair. I even have to pay a Filipino boy to come in and clean up the house. As for letters ..." He shook his head wryly. "Why, in my position, I learned long ago not to put anything down in black and white."

"Bellew got some nasty letters from somebody who knew all about your daughter's death."

"Quite a few people knew all about her death," the old man said slowly. "All except the names of the men involved. My wife was quite a talker. Didn't go out much. Stayed at home and chatted with the neighbors. You might remember this, though. Bellew was the one put me into the way of getting rich. I wouldn't want to scare him or worry him. When he handed me that money, those few thousands, it was like a great light breaking for me. I finally had something to sell. All my life, poor as dirt, working like a dog, a woman and child around my neck like millstones." He licked his parchment lips. "And then I had something to sell: I had grief. I had a father's natural grief and hatred for the men who had hurt my child. I'll tell you—getting me calmed down was a mighty expensive proposition."

"I can imagine," Warne said. The old man seemed to Warne so completely evil and despicable that he got up from the chair and moved away, putting the width of the room between them. "Why did you send James to beat me up? Why did my visit here scare you so?"

"I know the heirs are after the money," Mr. Gordon said. "And James … well, he's in such good shape it seems a shame not to let him practice a bit now and then. He goes to the gym. But that's like playing."

"The next time he tackles me," said Warne with his hand on the door, "I'm going to shoot him in the guts. Tell him so, when he's patched up and feeling better."

Sandra came down the steps of the secretarial school and saw Warne waiting in the car, and seemed both pleased and astonished at finding him there. Warne got out and opened the car door. "How about lunch?"

"You'll spoil me!" She got into the car. Warne went around and slid back in behind the wheel. "How on earth did you find me?"

"Aunt Faye. She said I could catch you when classes let out."

"I have to be at work by one-thirty."

"Yes, I know. The Building and Loan."

"How about a sandwich in a drive-in? I wish I had more time— but I don't."

Warne tooled the car away from the curb. "How about marrying me? And quitting work?"

She laughed a little. "I wish you meant it."

"How do you know I don't?"

She was suddenly serious. "I guess I don't. Do you mean it, Ed?"

"You're damned right." My God, he'd proposed to her in the bold- est way possible! Why in hell couldn't he have waited for a little romantic moonlight and music? I'm a cluck, he thought disgustedly. Proposing to my woman on a street full of traffic, with my hands full of steering wheel. "I ought to have my rear end kicked in," he said savagely.

"Why?"

"This." He motioned at the hurrying traffic, the clot of pedestrians at the corner, the mildly run-down little business section. "It isn't the place I meant to choose."

She put a hand on his. "It's a very pretty place, Ed, when the man you love has just asked you to marry him."

They went into a small cafe and picked a booth at the rear, and Warne kissed her. She wasn't bashful or afraid to be seen kissing him there. She was relaxed, giving freely of herself and her affection. When the waitress came, she gave an order calmly.

When the meal was almost over, Warne said, "I've got to ask you something. I have a hunch you may not want to answer."

There was a slight dimming of the glow in her eyes. "Well—go ahead and ask."

"The other day," Warne began, wondering how best to put it, "in the office talking to Bellew, I noticed that you reacted when he mentioned the odor of moth-balls. You remember—he'd come back late, and someone had entered the office, and left the smell there. He thought, to frighten him. But it seemed to mean something to you, too."

Her eyes dropped. She sat quite still. Then she shook her head. "I ... I don't feel that I have a right to mention what came into my mind. It's just guessing, just a coincidence."

"Perhaps not." He waited, but she seemed too troubled and uneasy to go on, so he added: "Was it about Aunt Faye?"

After a moment's hesitation she nodded slowly. "I'd better tell you. It can't mean anything. But you'd be better able to decide, perhaps. On that day Aunt Faye had taken some clothes out of storage, out of a box in the garage, some old things she hadn't intended to wear again. But among them she had found a skirt she used to like a lot. When I came after Dotty that night, she had it on. It smelled to high heaven of moth balls. I told her about it, but she brushed it aside. You see, since she'd gotten older, her sense of smell isn't very keen."

"She didn't realize how strong the smell was?"

"I'm sure she didn't."

He knew that the conversation was hurting Sandra, disturbing her. But he had to continue. "Did you accuse her? Or was that fight between you over something. else?"

"I accused her. She became hysterical. Then I thought, I must be wrong. She's been so kind to Dotty and to me. She wouldn't do a thing like writing those letters to Mr. Bellew."

"I'm not so sure. Don't blame yourself for the quarrel—yet. How would Aunt Faye be able to get into the office, if she had gone there?"

"I've lost a couple of keys, since I started work. Or at least, I thought I had. If it were Aunt Faye, of course—" Sandra was plucking at a paper napkin, tearing it nervously and rolling the bits between her fingers. "No, there must be some other explanation!"

"Do you mind if I go talk to her? Could I go now? Would Dotty be taking a nap?"

Sandra nodded. "Yes, Dotty would be napping now." She lifted her eyes to him. "If you go—be kind to her, will you?"

"I promise."

They went out, back to the car, and Warne delivered her to the door of the Building-Loan office.

Aunt Faye answered her door promptly. She didn't seem at all overjoyed to see Warne in person, though she had answered civilly enough earlier over the phone. She wore the usual high-necked black cotton blouse, a full black skirt. "Couldn't you find Sandra at the school?" she demanded.

"Yes, I found her. We had lunch together."

Aunt Faye stood with her hand on the knob, blocking the doorway, her attitude plainly one of, well, what do you want now? Warne added, "I want to talk to you about something which concerns just ourselves."

She flicked her eyes out to the car, as if trying to see whether he had brought anyone with him. She moved backward with an air of unwillingness. "Come in, then. Dotty's sleeping. We'll have to be quiet."

"I'll be quiet." I wish to God, Warne added to himself, that I didn't have to say a word. "May I sit down?"

"I don't allow smoking," she said primly. She sat down without touching her back to the back of the chair. She sniffed once or twice, folded her hands in her lap. "If you have some idea of asking my permission to marry Sandra, it isn't necessary at all. She's grown up, married before, a child too—both of you know what you're doing."

"I love Sandra. She's agreed to marry me." He paused, letting her see that the conversation was not to concern these things. "This is about some anonymous letters written to a friend of mine, a man named Bellew."

Nothing changed in her iron face, but Warne noted the tightening of the knobby hands on her lap. They clenched like claws until she remembered to relax. She moved uneasily on the chair. "I know all about Mr. Bellew. Sandra has worked for him for a year or more."

"I know you've heard of him from her. Did you know, too, that a long time ago he was indirectly responsible for the death of a young girl?"

She choked off a gasp. "Well, is that so?"

"Of course, nobody in his right mind could really blame Bellew for what happened. The girl misrepresented herself. She told Bellew she was older than she actually was. She let him think she'd had experience."

A sharp light glittered in her eyes. She moved her hands from her lap, gripping the arms of her chair. "That's no excuse!"

"The parents forgave him." He waited, but her manner was watchful. He still didn't have her off guard. "There was no reminder whatever of this girl's death until fairly recently, when the letters started. I thought, as Bellew did, that they might have been sent by the parents. But the mother is dead—"

She caught her breath sharply and her gaze wavered.

Warne said softly, "You liked her pretty well, didn't you?"

She turned her head so she wouldn't face him. "Yes, I liked her."

"Where did you know them? Was it while they were living in the little house near Griffith Park?"

"I lived next door," Aunt Faye admitted, almost in a whisper.

Warne crossed his legs. He wished he might have had a cigarette. He rubbed a hand across his chin. She wouldn't meet his eyes now but her manner had lost some of its stony enmity. "Bellew had the letters examined by a document expert. The letters were typed on a new machine. Probably by a woman. The sheets were regular high-grade social correspondence paper but the envelopes had an interesting story to tell."

One of her hands fluttered out to touch a small table by her side, to straighten a doily on it.

"The envelopes aren't made any more," Warne continued. "They were made some time ago by a paper firm as a sort of experiment. Whoever uses them has access to a store of out-of-date stationery."

Her eyes moved around to settle on his face. "I know what you're getting at, Mr. Warne. Sandra told you about the moth-ball smell, too, didn't she? And I've rented a new typewriter. But even so—"

"Wouldn't you like to tell me about it?" he suggested calmly. "It must be a load on your conscience. Some things have happened that demand explaining. Serious things."

She looked down at her lap, coloring a little. "I wrote the letters."

Warne said, "You were afraid for Sandra? Is that why you began?"

"I was a fool, I didn't trust her. I thought perhaps he'd manage to coax her to go on a party like the Gordon girl. And something bad might happen to her, Dotty left all alone lust me to care for her, an old woman on a miserable little pension—" She broke off, biting her lips. "I ... I used some pretty bad language in those letters," she admitted regretfully.

Warne grunted. "You just about scared Bellew to death."

"I tried and tried, but I couldn't make Sandra believe she shouldn't work there. I see now, my fears were foolish. But at first I was haunted by what I knew about the Gordon girl...." She suddenly covered her face, and Warne wondered if she were about to break down. But almost at once she straightened in her chair, lifted her face, turned her eyes to his. Her mouth was a little crooked and tight, the colorless lips pressed into a pencil-sharp line. "I might as well admit it all. I used to go to Bellew's office at night. Just once in a while. I'd disarrange his desk or leave lights on. I didn't damage anything. I had a key, one that Sandra had left here by accident, and I was careful about avoiding the cleaning women."

He said, "Well, now, since the letters prophesied that another girl would die as Janie Gordon had died—what about Candy Carroll?"

"I had nothing to do with that, of course," she said promptly, looking Warne right in the eye.

CHAPTER SIXTEEN

"You called your shots mighty close to be using a scatter gun," Warne said, watching her closely, trying to read her face.

Her expression didn't change by one whit. "It's the truth, though, I wrote the letters to scare Mr. Bellew, to keep him from sending any inexperienced girls out to those dirty parties. I was thinking mostly of Sandra, of course. But when the murder happened—"

"Wait a minute. There's been nothing definite in the papers, that it was murder."

"It was, though. Mr. Bellew showed the letters to somebody and they saw a chance, making a threat come true. I played right into a murderer's bands. I'm sorry for it." She didn't look sorry. She looked like a grounded vulture, sighing over a heap of bones.

Warne said suddenly, "Hell, it's as plain as day. You killed that girl."

"Why should I?"

In the instant's silence that followed her question, Warne heard a car door slam outside. He got up quickly and went to a window. Sandra was hurrying up the walk, a cab was pulling away from the curb. In another moment Sandra rapped quickly and then opened the door and stepped in.

She looked at Warne. "I couldn't stay away. I had to know!" Her glance flicked from him to the gaunt old woman across the room.

"She's admitted writing the letters," Warne told her. "She was worried for fear Bellew might use you in his business. Or so she says."

Sandra stood silent. She appeared dazed, confused. "Oh, no!"

"It wasn't any surprise," Warne said. "Bellew and I already had a few clues. The envelopes in which the letters were mailed had come from an old stock, something not even made any more. And you said your aunt had had a stationery store, and that your uncle was a sucker for salesmen with odd-lots to get rid of."

He saw disbelief begin to seep from Sandra's eyes, to be replaced by the bitter realization of the truth.

"The principal hint we had was that the sheets of letter paper had been handled by a small child. The other day when I saw the papers Dotty carried, the ones she'd used to draw pictures ... well, I knew then. There was just one other person who might have been responsible for the letters. Or I guess I should say, that I hoped could be responsible."

Sandra went over to sit near her aunt. Aunt Faye seemed even less worried and downcast than before. She seemed to have cheered up with Sandra's arrival.

"Aunt Faye, I'm terribly sorry. I wish I'd never gone to work there ... except—" Her eyes went to Warne. *Except, I'd never met you,* they told him.

"Do you know what he wants me to admit to, now?" Aunt Faye said briskly. "Murder, no less!"

"Murder?" Sandra whispered.

"I haven't used the word. I mentioned Candy Carroll's death. It has seemed to me from the beginning that the letters must have had some bearing on her dying as she did. Suicide or murder. Or accident. Isn't it possible you went to see Miss Carroll with the idea of turning her from her footloose ways," he said directly to Aunt Faye, "and that you had a slight argument?"

Sandra was suddenly roused to anger, on her feet, a spot of color burning in each cheek. "Aunt Faye wouldn't harm a soul! Anything she did—yes, even writing those letters—she did from the kindest of motives!"

Warne answered dryly, "She could have gone to see Miss Carroll with the noblest thoughts on earth. It wouldn't have kept them from struggling near that window."

Sandra said in a heated, rising voice, "And what about this second attack? The papers link it to the other. Did Aunt Faye waylay Chickie Anderson on a dark street and tear her clothes off? Leave her naked for some stranger to find?"

He knew she was getting mad at him. His glance skipped to the old lady. She looked pretty smug and triumphant, he thought, now that Sandra was here to defend her. He studied the big competent hands folded on her lap, the strong wrists, the sinewy build inside the harsh black dress. Physically she should be able to tackle a soft little doll like Chickie, like biting into a marshmallow.

"I don't know," Warne said. "I wish I didn't have this feeling, this hunch, that the letters must have something to do with what happened to those girls. I won't believe in coincidences." He appealed to the old lady. He hated to have this quarrel with Sandra, have her angry with him, over this prim and narrow-minded aunt. "Won't you admit the whole truth?"

"I've told you the truth." Her teeth clacked as she shut her mouth. Her hatchet-like face beamed with victory. "I'll say no more."

Warne thought to himself, "I'm licked if I stay here and keep fighting them. Sandra will hate me. She'll never get over it, never forgive me, even if it turns out I'm right. Most of all, if I'm right. He said as if giving up the point, "I'll have to look around and see what I can find out from other people."

"Go to the police," Sandra commanded, "and find out what they're doing. You'll get a whole new slant, and it won't be on Aunt Faye!"

"Don't go to the police," Aunt Faye corrected quickly. "There's no call to mention me to them."

"I wasn't going to," Warne said ironically, heading for the door.

At the apartment house, Warne stepped from the car and sized up the place. Not too exclusive he thought, but a little better than average. It had a pretty good view out over the valley's end, towards Glendale.

Ho went into the lobby and looked around. There was a desk, a bell on the wall where one could ring for the manager. He pushed the button and waited. The landlady came out of a door at the back of the hall. Warne sized her up. In spite of the silly color she had dyed her hair, she had a manner of common sense and alert eyes. Warne said, "I wonder if you'd mind answering a few questions about Miss Carroll's death?"

"My goodness," she said, "that's ancient history now. Everybody who's been here this morning wants to know all about Chickie Anderson."

"I suppose so. Well, of course I'm interested in that, too."

"Poor Miss Anderson! Here we were, right where you and I are now; standing and talking not more than a half-hour before that fiend ripped off all her clothes!" She glanced around the lobby as if taking in the scene of a crime. Then she said to Warne: "Now, what are you—a police detective?"

"I'm an insurance investigator," Warne said, offering her one of his business cards.

She read it, then handed it back to him. "I see. Well, perhaps we'd better go to my apartment to talk. It'll be more private there." To her, Warne's business had obviously given him official status.

Warne followed her down the hall, and she threw open a door for him to enter. The apartment was rather crowded with old-fashioned furniture. She offered Warne a chair and he sat down.

She began promptly, "Miss Carroll was just a visitor, staying with Chickie Anderson. I'd never met her. If she was anything like Miss Anderson, though, she must have been a real nice girl. Miss Anderson has been here for about two years and there never was a nicer tenant."

"Had Miss Carroll had any contacts with other tenants?"

"I don't think so."

"I guess the police explored any chance of a quarrel between the two girls?"

"Oh, yes, that seemed to be the first idea to pop into their heads. They asked me all about it, was Miss Anderson on the outs with her friend. But then they checked on the time and Miss Anderson couldn't have been here when her friend killed herself."

Warne said, "The papers this morning are giving a big play to a new theory. It wasn't suicide, it was murder."

She shook her head. "I hadn't heard that." She started to frown. "I hate to think of it like that. Suicide's bad enough. And then, I thought that business of the crazy laughter ... Mrs. Hackendyke's story, you know. Well, it fitted, in with the idea of suicide. The girl was alone and something upset her and she sort of went out of her mind."

"She could have been laughing at something, or someone."

She nodded. "Well, that was Miss Anderson's idea. We were talking about it just before she left early for her job."

"Left early?" Warne asked.

"Someone telephoned. Mrs. Macklin was just leaving Chickie's place at the time. She overheard. Someone called her, wanted her to come early to the club. Something about a change in the show Miss Anderson was doing."

"It could have been a trap," Warne said slowly. "Getting her out there when no one else was apt to be around."

"I told the police."

"You said Miss Anderson had some theory about this laughter. What was it?"

A puzzled, frustrated expression came into the manager's eyes. "I wish I knew. She said something about an old lady at a bus stop," the manager remembered suddenly. "I'm sure of that much."

Warne felt his heart drop. "An old lady? Could Miss Anderson describe her?"

"Yes, she did. She said the old lady was awfully prim and old-. fashioned, that you knew just by looking at her she'd never kicked up her heels a bit. Repressed is what they call it now. Do you get my meaning?"

"I think so." In Warne's mind was the image of Aunt Faye, hatchet-faced, the air of generalized disapproval thick enough to cut with a butter knife.

"As I recall, Miss Anderson said that she and Miss Carroll were waiting at a bus stop when this old lady got to talking to them. And something about this character just sent Miss Carroll into hysterics. Well, I guess if you believed Mrs. Hackendyke's story, it would make you stop and think."

"It sure would," Warne agreed. "What happened, finally? I mean, between these two girls and the proper old woman?"

"I didn't get the end of it."

"Did Miss Anderson speak of it as if they might have met the old lady since? That she might have looked them up?"

"Well ... I couldn't say. Aren't you going to see Miss Anderson in the hospital? You could ask her about it then."

"I doubt if the police would let me in."

"I could go, I guess," she said a little doubtfully. "The hospital called not long ago. Miss Anderson is conscious and wants some things from her apartment. Some of those shortie gowns she likes, and some cosmetics. The makeup in her handbag was trampled and ruined."

"I'll drive you to the hospital."

The landlady made up her mind. "All right, then. I'll go up and get a few of her things together. Wait for me in the lobby, will you?"

Warne waited beside the front entry. He tried to control his nervousness by smoking the cigarettes Aunt Faye had forbidden. If through his actions the old woman's head went into a noose, he knew that Sandra would never forget it. I ought to stop right here, he thought suddenly. No one but Bellew and I and a few other people who won't talk, know about those letters the old woman wrote. The cops don't seem to have an inkling.

He knew now why no tip-off had reached the papers. Aunt Faye was lying low.

If I keep my mouth shut, he told himself, and if I stay away from this Chickie Anderson and the story of some old woman at a bus-stop, things will die down in time. Sandra and I can get married. She can stay home and take care of Dotty, and we can gradually lose contact with the aunt.

He groaned to himself. The temptation was overpowering. He threw the cigarette out upon the sunny sidewalk and turned to the entry. At that moment the landlady appeared, carrying a small suitcase that must be Chickie's, a brown coat over her dress and a green straw hat squashed down over the pinkish hair. "Well, I'm ready. Here we go, Mr. Warne."

Warne tried to say, "I'm not going with you," but the words didn't emerge. It would be useless to try to shut the question out of his mind. It would never let him alone. Not even Sandra's love could silence it.

At the hospital, they enquired at the general desk and were directed to the fourth floor, west. In the west wing, when they reached it, they found the corridor guarded by a big counter and PBX switchboard, several nurses there working on charts and answering phone calls. Warne and the apartment manager waited until a large important-looking woman in a white uniform and cap, took notice. She was obviously the one in command.

"Miss Chickie Anderson?" She frowned, looking at them closely. "Yes, I know she has requested things brought from home." A moment of waiting, then, while she considered. But then the supervisor said, "Down the hall, room four twenty-six. Don't stay long."

A man who had been standing at a phone in a niche on the wall now turned around and took a good look at them. It was Robinson, the reporter. His gaze slid over Warne, stopped at his eyes; and then Robinson winked. He said in a rather loud tone to the supervisor: "Why won't you let the press in, then, Miss?"

With an air of prim rebuke, as though Robinson was a little boy caught picking his nose, the supervisor said, "I've explained, Mr. Robinson, that Miss Anderson doesn't care to see any reporters. She blames what happened to her on some story which appeared in a newspaper. She wants nothing more to do with people like you."

"My God, I'm just trying to make an honest living!" Robinson cried, as if deeply hurt.

"I would much prefer that you make it somewhere else," the supervisor replied, her tone taking on some iron. "We can't have hospital routine disrupted here."

"If I told everything I knew—" Robinson went on grumbling as he stepped over to the elevators. He wanted Warne to see that he was keeping his mouth shut as a favor.

Walking down the hall towards Chickie's hospital room, Warne expected at any moment to be called back to the desk to explain his business. Surely the police had stressed the danger of allowing casual visitors. Then Warne took a good look at the landlady beside him. Pink hair or not, there was definitely a no-nonsense air about her. Rugged honesty and hard work had left their mark. She wasn't the type to sneak a fiend in to have a second chance at the girl. Warne relaxed.

The landlady rapped on the closed door and a nurse said, "Come in." Warne followed the bobbing green hat into the dimness of the hospital room and saw the girl against the pillows, and felt hot shock run through him. A lot of her was hidden by bandages, but still he could see the terrible bruises, the swollen black eyes, the puffed distorted nose. In that instant Warne quit caring at all who was hurt by what Chickie Anderson knew.

Let her spill it and the devil take the hindmost.

CHAPTER SEVENTEEN

The landlady walked over without hesitation and patted Chickie's limp hand. "Why, you're looking almost as good as new!" she cried.

Chickie's eyes strayed over towards him. "Who's he?"

"Mr. Warne. He's with the insurance people. Wanted to talk for just a minute, if it won't tire you."

"Insurance?" Chickie hitched herself against the pillows, turning her puffed eyes fully to Warne. "Hospital insurance? I don't have any, as far as I know. Unless Mr. Spencer at the club—"

"It's about Miss Carroll."

"Oh." Chickie relaxed a little. "Poor old Candy. Say, will you make it kind of short, though? My jaw hurts like fury when I talk."

"Poor kid," said the landlady. "Look, I brought your things. I'll be hanging them in the closet while you talk to Mr. Warne."

Warne moved over nearer the bed, aware of Chickie's close and faintly suspicious scrutiny. "The thing I'm hoping to clear up is this mad laughter detail. It seems to have no connection with anything else in the case. No one heard it, apparently, but this one woman, Mrs. Hackendyke."

Chickie nodded, holding her bandaged jaw gingerly. "Yes, I know."

"Your manager was telling me that in talking to her you said you'd had some sort of contact with an old woman at a bus stop, and that somehow this proper, repressed kind of person caused Miss Carroll to go off into gales of laughter."

Again she nodded. "It was embarrassing."

"Could you describe this woman?"

"Oh, she was old, awfully old," Chickie said weakly. "And sort of futzy looking, if you know what I mean. Old-fashioned and proper. But it wasn't the way she looked that made Candy laugh like crazy. It was what she said."

"She disapproved of you and Miss Carroll, perhaps?" Warne guessed, thinking of Aunt Faye and her outspoken propriety.

"Oh, I don't think so! She didn't know anything about us," Chickie said. "It was this yarn she told, the experience she'd had with a man in a park at night." Chickie giggled. "You could tell, the way she told it to us, she really had no idea at all what this man had wanted. She was such an innocent old doll. No experience with men. She'd been walking her little dog on the street and this man had come up to her and told her his own dog was in the park, sick, and would she come and take a look." Chickie paused to touch her bandages and flinch.

"You know what he was?" Chickie muttered horsely. "He was a mugger. A rapist. He got the little old lady off behind some bushes and pulled off about half her clothes and threw her down on the ground. And then—" In sudden embarrassment, Chickie looked away towards the windows. "I can't remember the words she used. She had such a weird idea of what had really happened, anyway. She was afraid he was trying to steal the dog. The dog was worth fifty dollars, she told us."

Warne waited, sensing the nurse's impatience. He had abandoned all hope that this irrelevant tale had anything to do with Candy Carroll's death. There was nothing here for him. The landlady's kindly effort had been in vain, after all.

"He couldn't," Chickie said abruptly, breaking the moment of silence.

"He couldn't?" Warne echoed, not understanding.

"No. After all the tricks, getting the old lady off alone and tying the dog to a bush, and fighting to tear off her clothes—he wasn't able to do what he wanted. Don't you see?" She waited for Warne to catch on. "It was *him*."

"I see what you mean," Warne said slowly, "but when Miss Carroll—"

"That's what Candy was splitting her sides about."

It dawned on him. The complete picture. Well, Candy Carroll had shared this particular point of humor with a lot of other women.

"I'll be damned." Warne grinned to himself. As a man, he found perhaps somewhat less humor in the item than Candy had. But he could understand her viewpoint. Born to tease, he reminded himself. To a girl in Candy's provocative trade, the predicament of the mugger in the park might have seemed hilariously funny. "So that's what tickled her funny bone."

"Candy always thought anything like that was a scream," Chickie replied. "I thought she'd laugh herself sick, that time. The old lady must have thought she was crazy."

The nurse came forward firmly into the middle of the room. "I think it's time Miss Anderson rested, now. Give her a couple of days of complete quiet, then come see her again."

Next step would be to call the orderlies, Warne knew. He turned for the door. The landlady had hung up Chickie's garments, put the small case on the floor of the closet. She followed Warne into the hall. There she straightened the green hat on her head, and said with a hint of awkward apology, "Well, that wasn't much of a story she had to tell, after all. And not such a nice one. I'm surprised, Miss Carroll found it so funny."

"If Candy Carroll was laughing her head off just before she fell from that window—"

They exchanged a glance, surmising on Warne's part and embarrassed on hers. "Oh, I don't think anything like that would have been going on," she said quickly.

On one hand he had Aunt Faye, glibly denying that she'd had anything to do with the death that had so exactly followed out the prophecy in her letters. On the other hand ... he recalled Bellew's blurted remark, *He made it happen!*" Meaning, the writer of the letters. And this remark had stayed with Warne because it so exactly mirrored what was in his own mind.

He still didn't believe in tea leaves. He still couldn't let it go as coincidence. But he might as well drop the angle of Aunt Faye and look elsewhere for the connection. Chickie's story of the old lady at the bus stop had blown up into a ludicrous joke. It had nothing to do—

He checked that line of thought abruptly.

As they passed through the lobby of the hospital, Robinson came from a waiting room and fell into step beside Warne. "How about a break, huh? I didn't queer your game up there."

Warne didn't stop. "Don't you feel a little guilty about getting Miss Anderson almost killed with that story you made up?"

"I won't kid you, kid," Robinson said dryly. "I feel bad about it. I want to do something nice for the girl. Look, a little more publicity might do her a world of good. Tell me what you went to see her about. How's about it?"

"What I went to see her about fizzled into nothing at all," Warne said. "But I might have something for you, at that. A strange footnote to the death of Candy Carroll."

They had come to the door and Robinson was inclined to hang back. Plainly he thought Warne had nothing much for him. "Oh, is that so?" As the landlady stepped out through the door, he half turned. "Nothing on Chickie Anderson?"

"Nothing about Chickie. But this is right up your alley. Wouldn't you like a yarn about a mysterious old man whose wealth is based on a rape, a suicide, and blackmail?"

Robinson stopped moving. "All in one story? My, my! Who is this fascinating character?"

"A man named Josiah Gray Gordon."

Robinson was watching him thoughtfully. "Never heard of the guy."

"He has a big place on the beach near Malibu. Exclusive. Keeps a tough young bodyguard. The bodyguard has a beautiful, broad-minded wife."

"Now you're warming up. What's the pitch? Anything to do with what I'm working on now?"

"The connection is priceless," Warne said as if he were handing Robinson a brace of oriental pearls. "Here's how it stacks up. More than twenty years ago a seventeen-year-old girl named Janie Gordon needed money for dancing lessons. She went to Bellew's office and asked for a party date. She lied about her age, and she was a mature girl, and Bellew sent her out on a job. A smoker. The lodge brothers got drunk, and the party got rough. Janie Gordon was raped by three men whose names are known only to her father. On the following Sunday morning she jumped out of a high window in downtown L.A."

"That'll be in the files," Robinson commented to himself.

Warne went on: "The father's name was Josiah Gray Gordon. Bellew was so guilt-stricken he sold his agency and gave the money to the parents. Within a short time they'd made two moves. Big ones."

"What happened to the mother?"

"She died, not too long after the girl did. It's the old man who'll reward any interest you show in him."

Robinson grinned wickedly. "He's going to hate me."

"There won't be anything in the newspaper morgue about the rape, since the old man kept quiet for a price. A big price. But you'll have a legitimate reason to drag it all up and speculate about it in print. The Janie Gordon death looks like an exact pattern for Candy Carroll's jumping out that window. I guess you'll know what to do about that."

Robinson put his hand on Warne's sleeve. "I'm writing a new will today. I'm leaving you everything I own. My office shears and paste-pot. A second-hand brownie camera. Two tickets to Disneyland. And my interest in a crepe paper monkey." His grip tightened. "But really, pal—and I do mean pal—if this pans out I'll stand you a dinner anywhere you name."

"Good luck," Warne said, and went outside to where the landlady was waiting for him.

On the drive back to the apartment house, she was pretty quiet. On the steps, bidding Warne goodbye, she said, "I guess I'd better crack down on guests coming to stay with my tenants. I'm sort of particular who I let in here."

"I doubt if you'll have any more visitors flying out of windows," Warne assured her. "This one was just a fluke."

"Gives the place a bad name. Did you tell that reporter what Miss Anderson said? About what made Candy Carroll laugh so hard?"

"I didn't tell him."

"Thanks." She started in, then looked back. "It doesn't necessarily mean she had someone up there with her, does it?"

He hated to disappoint her. "I'm afraid it does."

"And she was laughing at him?"

Warne was turning back to the car. "Miss Carroll was blessed with a fabulous sense of humor."

He drove to the office just off Sunset, went into the building and climbed the stairs, unlocked his door for the second time that day. Warne sat down behind his desk, relaxing in his chair, and looked at the reports on his desk, work to be done. He had no taste for it now. He was oppressed by a sense of let-down, of his own unbelievable thick-headedness. He needed a drink.

There was a pint, almost full, in one of the filing cabinets. He mixed Scotch with a splash of water from the cooler.

He was at the window, looking at the street below, the paper cup almost empty in his hand, when the phone rang. He crossed to the desk, lifted the receiver off its cradle. Bellew's voice was a crack of sound, popping inside his ear. "Some damned reporter just called me," Bellew stuttered, "and asked about the Janie Gordon case. He had all the records! My God, Warne, they've finally got onto it!"

"What did you tell him?"

"I denied everything, of course. Look, did you see Gordon again?"

"This morning. By invitation, in a way." Warne tipped the paper cup and downed the last of the Scotch. "You'd better come right down here. We can talk in your office. Better than over the phone."

"What does Gordon want?"

"I'll tell you when I see you," and without saying goodbye or waiting for further word from Bellew, Warne replaced the phone.

He went around the desk and opened the wide top drawer and looked at the odds and ends collected in it. Lots of souvenirs. He took the steel ring from his coat pocket and dropped it among the others, the broken pens and unsharpened pencils, the rubber bands and old receipts for rent and office services, the Canadian coins he'd forgotten and brought back from Vancouver, the

cigarette lighter from Yokohama, carved walrus ivory from
Juneau, the tiny derringer he'd picked up years ago in a shop on
St. Peter Street in New Orleans. With a sudden wry tightening
of his lips he picked up the little gun and hefted it against his
palm, then slid it into his belt. He buttoned his coat over it.

He was at the head of the stairs as Bellew came up puffing, the
limp almost causing him to stumble, eyes like burned holes in a
gray face. Bellew unlocked his own door with a rattle of keys,
motioned Warne to step in, then shut the door behind them.
Bellew went quickly to the inner door, opened it, limped in and
around the desk. He sat down as if his legs were giving out. He
motioned towards a second chair for Warne.

"This thing, breaking now. I thought I was in the clear," he said
in a broken, panting voice.

"Far from it," Warne said.

"I can't understand how they suddenly dug up this Janie
Gordon suicide. Of course they'll play it up now, along with
Candy's death, and as far as any hope of staying in business,
running an agency, I'm through."

"If that's all you've got to worry about, you're in luck," Warne
said. "I thought you'd have more on your mind than the chance
of keeping an agency."

Bellew shook his head, waving a hand as if waving Warne's idea
away. "Tell me about Gordon."

"This creep he uses as a bodyguard has a wife. A real hot
number. She came here early today with a tale about Mr. Gordon
wanting some money out of you. It sounded enough like him,
judging by what I know, to have been true, so I bit. She suckered
me. All it was, Native Boy wanted a return match. His pride had
been hurt."

Bellew frowned in impatience. "What does Gordon want of
me?"

"When this story breaks in the paper's he's going to want your
scalp. He admitted the heirs of one of his victims were looking for
ways to take his money away from him. Mr. Gordon's been
nervous over his source of cash for quite a while. That's why he

checked up on you about a year ago, and why he's so eager to collect some legitimate cash from the insurance companies."

"This publicity will hurt him?"

"It won't do him any good. He's like something under a rock. He scuttles when the sunlight hits him."

Bellew sagged forward against the desk. "You called me down here to tell me this? For God's sake, I'm packing, I'm up to my neck in the details of sub-leasing my place and selling the furniture. Why drag me down on something like this?"

"I didn't call you to tell you about Gordon. Not really." Warne turned slightly in his chair, his hand flattening against his waist. "I wanted to hear your story, the real story, of the night Candy Carroll fell from that window."

He waited, and Bellew seemed about to speak; and then shut his mouth.

"Why did you kill her?" Warne asked softly.

CHAPTER EIGHTEEN

Bellew couldn't have looked worse if Warne had punched him in the solar plexis. "What are you saying? You're accusing me of murder?"

"No, not quite. You couldn't have had more than a moment or so of premeditation. I think you might cop a plea of manslaughter."

Bellew's hands made fluttering motions on the desk, finally settled on the phone. He licked his lips. "You want to call the police?"

"Not yet." Warne's air was easy and calm, willing to listen. "I want to hear your story first."

Bellew tried a ghastly imitation of a smile, "You've talked to someone else about this? Sandra, maybe?"

"Nobody."

The smile grew more confident. "I can't help you, Warne. I think you must have acquired some wrong ideas, somehow. Your reasoning must be warped."

"It all stacks up, right from the beginning. You supplied the background in your story about Janie Gordon. The trouble with your wife, the years of enforced quiet living, the repression. Being in your job, keeping hands off, forcing your mind off those girls, meant squeezing a sort of genie into a bottle—a bad genie—and keeping a tight cork in it. And then somehow and someday the cork blows out."

Bellew actually managed to laugh; "We're all repressed in one way or another. I just had to learn to leave the girls alone. After I got older, it didn't matter."

"It mattered, all right. The night you got a skinful of brandy, and went out to that clubhouse, and found out Candy Carroll hadn't been allowed to do what she loved ... which was to rouse men, tease them, bedevil them—that's the night your genie popped out of the bottle. A brandy bottle, shouldn't you say?"

Bellew had shrunk back into his chair. Between the untended sideburns his face seemed offended and sulky. "A man has a right to drink once in a while. So I had a few. I was nervous, wound up. So perhaps I might even have gone to check up on Candy. She was in a way my responsibility, and I had worries on my mind, those damned letters and what they kept saying might happen again."

Warne leaned towards Bellew without removing his hand from the front of his coat. "You betrayed yourself when you told me, 'He made it happen.' That short remark was like a great big light, Bellew, in the dark of that night Candy died. In the instant before you pushed her from that window, you remembered the letters and you knew that if the police ever really suspected you, you could tell them about the anonymous letter writer and make them think he'd committed the murder."

Bellew stood up abruptly. "You've forgotten one small detail, Warne, in the fairy tale about me and Candy Carroll. What possible motive could I have had for wanting to kill her?"

"The oldest in the world," said Warne, watching Bellew closely. "She insulted your manhood."

Bellew's face twitched; it was like the tearing of a mask. He was no longer the quiet, gray limping man Warne had known as an office neighbor. Something savage and lethal looked from his eyes.

"She laughed at you. And there was nothing you could do. You were paying the price of those years of guilt and repression."

"God damn you!" The words were incoherent, a bellowing cry, as Bellew sprang around the end of the desk in a single leap. He almost bowled Warne over. Waite hadn't had time to rise. He was pulling the derringer from his belt as Bellew landed. Bellew's weak flailing hands beat at his face, and Warne twisted sidewise, protecting himself with an arm thrown up. Bellew wasn't husky enough or skilled enough to hurt Warne much. He gave Warne's upheld arm a brief rattle of blows, and then flung himself off and ran panting and limping to the outer office. Warne had slipped to his knees. He jumped up now and started after Bellew.

"I thought you were my friend," Bellew threw back at him.

"Wait—" Warne wanted to say ... "I'm still your friend. I want to help you. For God's sake don't do anything silly." But there wasn't time and the words would only sound like a jumble of bad advice. He ran after Bellew. Bellew was forcing himself, trying to suppress the limp. He got halfway down the front stairs and then slipped and fell, and rolled the rest of the way. On the stairs, Warne saw Bellew regain his feet and stare around dazed, as if lost. "Bellew! Bellew, for God's sake—"

He ran towards the front entry. Warne ran down the steps and out—Bellew was already halfway down the block, towards Sunset Boulevard.

Some hint of Bellew's purpose reached Warne in that moment, and all he could think of was that Candy Carroll hadn't been worth it. Big, bosomy and beautiful ... she'd been a bitch, still, and Bellew was a fool if he intended what Warne thought he did. Warne tried to run faster, tried to think of something compelling to yell at the hurrying, limping man.

He heard the roar of a truck, getting into gear from the stop at the light, and he tried to push speed into his legs. Bellew was down at the corner now. He was looking towards his left, at the oncoming traffic, and a certain tense determination in him reached all the way back to Warne, trying to run in time to reach him; and Warne knew exactly what was coming next without being able to do a thing to stop it.

The truck came up with a roar of power and a clash of gears, a big tanker and trailer-tank full of gasoline, a juggernaut on unbelievable tires, with the driver high in his cab, remote, his eyes fixed on the next light two blocks beyond. Warne felt his throat clog. He was running out of wind, unable to breathe properly because he wanted to stop and yell. He waved an arm. Bellew didn't even look back.

At the last moment Bellew straightened his shoulders, forced himself quite erect, as if at the end he must give the appearance of a man, a real man about to die. Not afraid, not weak. Not the sort of man a girl like Candy Carroll would laugh at. Not a man to be made a fool of by a stripper. Not to be teased, then shown as a buffoon.

With head high, with shoulders back, Bellew stepped straight into the path of the truck. There was a sharp blast of a klaxon as, at the last moment, the driver caught some hint of motion just below. Then other cars let loose a whole cacophony, and Warne quit running. There was a scream of tires as the tanker's brakes locked on the asphalt. A gasp of breath like a puncture—too loud to be Bellew, and then a woman screamed.

Epitaph, Warne thought. There's always a woman around to scream goodbye.

It was almost dark in the office. Warne sat behind the desk. There was a bottle, the last of the pint, before him. A soggy paper cup. He didn't feel like going out to eat. He'd talked to the cops in the street, and in Bellew's office; and then the detectives from homicide. They'd already had a line on Bellew, it turned out; someone had described a man they'd glimpsed hanging about in the shadowy block below the Chatter Box. Bellew was the only one in the case who was small and gray and limped a little. The cops were getting ready to put a stakeout on Bellew, pull him in if he made a break. He wasn't the sort of man, Warne knew, who might have stood up under official questioning.

Better off dead. Warne said it to himself, tasting the bitterness of it and the uselessness. Bellew had come in perfect honesty to ask his help in running down the writer of the anonymous letters. And in the end, Warne's trail had led straight back to the man who had started him on it.

Warne got up and went over to the light switch. The room was getting dark. He might not be above drinking alone but damned if he'd drink in the dark, too. He had his hand on the switch when there was a rap at the door, and then it opened and in the dim light he saw Sandra.

"Ed? You're all alone here? I thought you must have gone—"

"I'm going pretty soon." He switched on the lights. His office looked bleak, he thought. Too much space for the few filing cabinets and the desk. Bellew's idea, dividing the room, was better.

Sandra came forward. She had her hair curled softly on her shoulders. No horn rims. She had on a blue cotton dress, cut low, no sleeves. She smelled clean. "Have you had dinner?" She was watching him anxiously.

"No. No dinner."

"A man named Robinson called me up about Mr. Bellew. Wanted some comment, and I didn't know anything to say."

"I'll bet he figured out something for you to say."

"No, he didn't. He said he knew I must feel confused. And that probably I hadn't had any idea Mr. Bellew was a murderer. Had killed Candy Carroll." She stood, twisting her white purse. "I still can't believe it. Why would he have killed her?"

Warne looked at her. She was beautiful, and he loved her; and he knew all at once that if he had found out Aunt Faye had killed half the people in Hollywood, he wouldn't have done anything about it, just for Sandra's sake. But he couldn't tell her why Bellew had had to kill Candy Carroll. She wouldn't have understood, and the crime would have shocked her. A man—it took a man to know why Bellew had pushed Candy Carroll out that window.

"He was funny, repressed little old guy," Warne said. "I guess he just went off his nut."

"He went to the apartment? To Miss Anderson's place?"

"Just to check up. He was worried." Full of brandy or not, Warne knew, Bellew must have gone up to Chickie's place with the best of intentions.

"Because of the letters?"

"Because of Aunt Faye's nasty letters," Warne said grimly. "Why don't you tell her? It might stop her, if she's ever tempted again."

Sandra nodded. "Yes, I'll tell her. I'm like you, Ed. I thought it might help straighten her out." Sandra came nearer. There was no doubt she felt some coldness on Warne's part. She said softly, "Do you blame me, in any way?"

"How could I?" He forced his thoughts off that last image of Bellew, stepping into the path of the truck. He put his hands on Sandra's shoulders and pulled her close, feeling her warmth, her freshness, the willingness of her response. She felt slim and smooth inside the blue cotton. Her flesh had a vital readiness that excited him. And then, there was this about Sandra: she had no intention of teasing. What she offered she offered cleanly, honestly. And what she seemed willing to give, she gave.

They kissed, and her mouth had none of the tricks of Madge Gordon's. There was just the honesty of love.

She drew back a little, still somewhat anxious, still concerned about him. She put up her fingers to touch his cheek. "What are you thinking about now?"

"I was thinking we'd better get married pretty quick. Say, next week. If not sooner."

"I'd like that."

"I'm pretty busy. We might put off the honeymoon."

"Who needs a honeymoon?" she said softly. "We can do everything at home."

It's going to be good, Warne thought. It's going to be very, very good.

THE END

If You See This Woman

By Dolores Hitchens

Junie's mouse-grey rump stuck out from under the marble-topped coffee table. She had spilled an ashtray, hitting it with the duster, and now there was a mess of ashes and cigarette butts to clean up. She was fumbling with the last of the butts when Mr. Arnold came into the room behind her. She knew that he must be looking at her; she heard him say, "What on earth are you doing? Laying an egg?"

She inched hastily backward, freeing her heavy shoulders from the rim of the table. She squatted, looking up at him, pink in the face from the exertion of stooping and crawling. "Oh, no, Mr. Arnold."

He grinned at her in the way she didn't understand. "Chasing a butterfly? Would you actually be chasing a butterfly, Junie?"

"Oh, no, sir." Junie got to her feet, tugged down the cotton uniform, reached for the fallen duster and the ashtray. "No, I wouldn't do that, Mr. Arnold."

"I know—you were dictating a letter to the little man who lives under the rug. A love letter."

She shook her head, speechless now, backing away gingerly. She wanted to swallow; her throat ached with the nervous need to swallow; but under Mr. Arnold's malevolent grin her throat had dried up.

Mrs. Arnold came into the room from the hall to the bedrooms. "Junie, the baby needs changing." Mrs. Arnold had on the pink satin jump suit, gold slippers, and wore her hair piled on top of her head, all silky darkness and pink ribbons. She looked beautiful. She looked like a doll Junie had once seen in a store window.

Mr. Arnold had put his briefcase on the coffee table and was lighting a cigarette. Mrs. Arnold looked at the briefcase. "You're really selling the stock today?"

"Dumping it. Dumping every damned share. Willcutt is in with me, he's selling his too. Then we'll both buy it back for next to nothing."

Mrs. Arnold went to the wall and straightened a picture there. She turned around. Junie was almost at the door to the hall. Mrs. Arnold said to her husband, "Well, just be careful what you're getting rid of, just don't throw out the baby along with the bath water."

Junie hurried down the hall. The words rang in her ears. Mr. and Mrs. Arnold were always saying strange things, but this thing that Mrs. Arnold said every once in a while was the strangest and the scariest of all. Who would throw out a baby in its bath? How could you make a mistake like that? Or ... could it mean that somebody might want to throw away a baby, might *want* to make it go down, down, down into the deep pipes, the lost places, the rushing water, the dark?

Junie shivered as she turned into the baby's room. Pete, almost a year old, was just beginning to stand well and to try to walk. He was a heavy, placid infant. Now he clung to the bars of the crib and gurgled as Junie rushed to him and put protective arms around him.

"Nice Petey."

At Sylvan Slopes Home no one had ever talked about throwing out a baby in its bath. You were taught carefully how to bathe a baby, along with how to dust and clean. But if you'd talked about throwing a baby away—Junie shook her head, trying to imagine the consequences of saying a thing like that at Sylvan Slopes.

They'd have sent you away—the principal, Mr. Willoughby, and the directress of instruction, Miss Gombie. They'd have given you a blue suitcase like the one you got when you were ready to graduate, and maybe some extra underwear, and a Bible, and

$10. And maybe Miss Gombie might have cried—that a girl of hers had said a thing like throwing a baby away, sneaky-like, in its bath water.

Junie could see it all in her mind, see it quite clearly. She wondered where a girl could go in such a case. Where would you run to? She couldn't imagine.

She tickled Petey gently, got him to lie down, opened his rompers, and changed the didy. Then, since he was obviously all through with his nap, she put him in his playpen. For a while she squatted beside the pen, handing him toys which he threw at her, and once in a while reaching gently to touch the dark curls that covered his head.

"My Petey. My own Petey."

She whispered the words, glancing guiltily at the door to the hall. Miss Gombie had been firm. You must never, never forget that the babies belonged to somebody else. To their parents. Even if their parents had adopted the baby. There had been one whole lesson on just that alone—Miss Gombie had taught it herself. Standing in front of the class in her green suit.

"We must love the children. All of our girls here love children. All of our graduates are famous for loving children," Miss Gombie had said in her forceful way. "We love them but we don't *possess* them."

There had been a short, puzzled silence.

"We don't own them," Miss Gombie said, and the word *own* made her mouth round and funny-looking, as if she were getting ready to suck an orange.

Her listeners had nodded their understanding.

For several days Mr. Arnold went around whistling and snapping his fingers, when he was home; and Mrs. Arnold bought a fur jacket and two new hats. At dinner they talked about a new car. They seemed very critical of the car, and yet while she served, and listened, it seemed to Junie that they were going to buy it anyway.

Then for almost a week the house was quiet because Mr. Arnold didn't whistle or snap his fingers anymore. Mrs. Arnold took the fur jacket back to the store. The other store wouldn't take back the hats. They no longer talked about the car, but about thousands and thousands of dollars, more than Junie could understand, and about something Mr. Willcutt hadn't done.

When Mr. Arnold noticed Junie, he asked questions like, "You gonna save ol' Massa from de po'house, Junie-bug?" Or "Think they'll take me in at Sylvan Slopes? I'll wear a wig and look retarded."

But Junie had no idea how to answer these strange questions.

Then at the end of the week Junie began to notice how cross Mr. and Mrs. Arnold were getting with each other. One night at dinner Mr. Arnold threw his wineglass at the wall and made a splotch, and Mrs. Arnold screamed. She mad-screamed, not scared-screamed, and in the kitchen Junie choked on her fright.

Then, watching carefully, Junie saw how they both began to get cross with Petey. Not so much at first, but when Petey caught the sniffles and cried at night, Mr. Arnold would get up and walk around and smoke, and say things quiet-like to himself. And Mrs. Arnold would make Junie get up and go to Petey's room and sing to him, and put him on her shoulder while she rocked in the rocking chair.

Then Mr. Arnold put a cot in Petey's room and told Junie she had to sleep in there, though this was against the rules. Junie knew they'd signed a paper before she came, saying she must have a room of her own.

One night when Petey was whimpering and Junie wasn't awake yet to walk around and carry him—she was tired all the time now, and slept heavily—Mr. Arnold came and threw open the door and cursed. He called Petey a damn brat and he called Junie a lazy, feeble-minded slut. His words bounced off the walls like bullets, and Junie cowered in terror.

They didn't love Petey anymore. That was it.

He was sick now, and his face looked rough and red, and he cried a lot. There was no curl in his hair—it looked lank and had no shine to it; and his voice had turned into a hoarse croak.

The doctor came and left some medicine, and told Junie how often to give it to Petey. Mrs. Arnold didn't even come into the room while the doctor was there. She sat in the living room, holding a cigarette, and when the doctor went back in there, Junie heard her saying, "Bill, I don't know when we can pay you," and the doctor answering, "Oh, forget it. And chin up, Betty. Mark's been through worse than this and come out smelling like a rose."

Junie was faithful about giving the medicine, and about rubbing Petey with alcohol, and rocking him to keep him from crying. At times she would fall asleep in the chair, and only wake when Petey stirred. Mrs. Arnold didn't help at all. She smoked more and more, and stared out of the windows at the skyline, and spent a lot of time talking on the telephone with her mother.

Mr. Arnold came home earlier now. His face seemed thinner and paler. He drank more. And once while Junie was lighting the candles for dinner, bending close with the match, he said, "A vestal virgin. Tell me, how did your high priest—Mr. Willoughby—how did he initiate you virgins? With fire and incense?"

Junie looked at him and wished she might give a proper answer. "We weren't ever allowed to play with matches." For some reason this set Mr. Arnold off into hoots of laughter.

It was going to be winter before too long, but today was mild. The apartment felt overheated and stuffy. Junie served Mr. Arnold his toast and coffee, and took a tray to Mrs. Arnold in bed. Then she bathed Petey and dressed him in the blue rompers with the white collar. His nose was still red, his eyes puffy. She hugged him for a long minute before she set him down in his playpen.

Then she went back into the bathroom, Petey's own private bathroom, and bent to touch the outlet lever for the tub. She was stooped there when she heard the Arnolds in the hall. Mrs. Arnold must have got out of bed and met Mr. Arnold there while he was getting his overcoat at the hall closet.

Mrs. Arnold asked something that Junie didn't catch, and Mr. Arnold answered, "Willcutt made money out of my losses. He was supposed to be with me, but he cut my throat. Now I think I have a chance to get back at him."

Mrs. Arnold said, "So we're going to throw the baby out with the bath water. Is that it?"

Mr. Arnold seemed to get mad all at once. "You're damned right, we're throwing the damn baby out with the damn bath water and we damned well should have done it long before now."

Junie's hand, reaching for the lever, began to shake. She managed to touch the lever, though, and the cold metal sent a chill all the way up her arm and into her heart. Her heart felt like a lump of steel ten times bigger than her fist, a hundred times too big for her chest, pounding coldly there inside her.

"You're determined to go on with this?" Mrs. Arnold said.

"Yes, I am. Damned right I am."

The water began to swirl and growl down into the pipe. Junie stared at it. Pipes must be dark places. Far, far below the city, she remembered from somewhere, there were giant pipes like great dark caves. It would be cold there, cold and slimy, with awful gurgling echoes, with rats maybe. Junie had seen a woods rat once.

Who would want to put a baby into a place like that?

The thought scared her so that she ran back to be with Petey.

Mr. Arnold hadn't left yet. They were in the living room now; she could hear the murmur of voices.

She looked at Petey. He was playing with a rubber elephant, pulling one of its ears. Junie's heart pounded harder than ever. What should she do?

She had a telephone number in her suitcase; it was written on a piece of paper, pinned to the lining. Miss Gombie had told her, if anything bad ever happened to her, she was to dial Operator and give her the number and tell her that the call was collect.

Would they help about Petey? Was there anything Miss Gombie could do? Would Mrs. Arnold catch her using the phone and stop her?

Crouched beside Petey's pen, Junie began to cry.

An hour went by.

Junie wiped her eyes and tidied up Petey's bed, then went to the kitchen and washed up the breakfast things. She mopped the floor, not because it needed it, but because she thought she might try to use the kitchen phone extension. But then, when she peeped into the living room, she saw that Mrs. Arnold was already using the phone. Mrs. Arnold had on a white negligee, all fluffy, with gold embroidery; and her hair was tied up with a yellow ribbon. She looked hard and strange.

Junie went to her room and put on her coat. She stole back to Petey's room, put on his cap and coat and leggings, and took an extra blanket. Then she remembered her purse. She could never remember exactly how much she still had left of the $10 they'd given her when she was graduated from Sylvan Slopes. Her money was put in the bank for her—the salary she was paid by the Arnolds. There was a little book that showed how much she had and every six months it had to be mailed to Sylvan Slopes, for some reason; but Junie had no idea of how she might get money out of the bank. Now, exploring her little change purse, she found $2.30.

There was money in the kitchen, though, in a funny small jar shaped like a beehive. Mrs. Arnold called it "gin money" and Mr. Arnold called it "the devil's bankroll." Junie picked up the baby and the blanket, stuffed her small change purse into her coat pocket, and stole silently out to the kitchen. She found a ten-dollar bill and three one-dollar bills and two quarters in the beehive. She took it all.

She went out the back way. There was a service elevator here where the janitor took away trash and things, but Junie didn't quite know how to work it. And then too, she didn't want to be seen by the janitor. He might remember. So she carried Petey all the way down the stairs, eight flights, stopping to rest twice.

In the street she paused, bewildered. The day was grayer and cooler than it had seemed from inside the apartment. The trees in the park across the street looked bare and wind-bitten. Aimlessly, Junie walked for a few blocks.

Petey was very heavy. Her arms ached. She knew now that she should have brought the stroller.

Just at that moment she was passing an apartment house and a nice big carriage with a baby blanket in it was standing by the doorway. No one was around, though when Junie touched the cushion inside the carriage, she found it still faintly warm from the baby which had just been taken upstairs. Sometimes Mrs. Arnold had taken Petey out, and had left the stroller for the janitor to bring in; and remembering this, Junie decided that's what had happened here.

She plopped Petey into the carriage and ran for the corner, turned the corner swiftly, then slowed to a walk.

Junie thought, I can be smart like anybody else when I have to be. She felt pleased with herself, alert, vigilant for Petey's welfare, on guard against the world.

After a random stroll of eight or nine blocks she turned back in the direction of the park. She and Petey spent several pleasant hours there. They sat on the grass and Petey patted some dead leaves into dust and then tasted his fingers. He stood up, clinging to Junie's shoulder, and when some fat squirrels ran past he tried to wobble after them.

When she began to feel hungry, Junie put the baby back into the carriage and they went south, toward another part of the city. They ate lunch in a restaurant where you put money in a slot and lifted a small glass door and took out the food. It was an easy way to buy what you wanted. She and Petey had two moist turkey sandwiches and two glasses of milk and four pieces of custard pie. Petey ate well, better than he had for days; the fresh air and the exercise must have been good for him.

Right after lunch Junie realized that she had made a serious omission; she had forgotten to bring diapers. But then she remembered: sometimes in an emergency, when the diaper service had been delayed, Mrs. Arnold had used a kind of disposable diaper that she said came from the drugstore.

D-R-U-G.

There one was. Junie went in, pushing the carriage. The person who waited on her let her change Petey in a room at the back of the store. The problem was solved.

She returned to the park. Petey took a nap, snug in the big warm carriage. He awoke later, and again was enchanted with the dusty leaves. But now it began to grow cold and windy. Junie thought over what she should do, and while she was thinking she noticed the buses running on the avenue next to the park.

She pushed the carriage out of sight, deep into some evergreen shrubs, and carrying Petey and his blanket and the package of disposable diapers, she went over to the bus stop. Ever since coming to the city she'd wanted to take a bus ride, but she'd never had the chance.

On the bus she sat in the back. Petey stood on the seat beside her, looking all around, making crowing and squealing noises. Several people noticed him, and smiled.

Junie took three different bus trips that afternoon, to various outlying parts of the city, seeing things she had never seen before. Coming back into downtown on the last trip, she noticed that twilight had drawn in and all the lights were on. It occurred to her that she and Petey had no place to sleep. Impulsively she turned to a middle-aged woman sitting beside her. "I'm going to have to find a room for the night," she said.

The woman looked at Petey and smiled. She coughed gently behind her hand. "Do you—uh—have any money?"

"Oh, yes. Well ... some."

The woman nodded and in a kind voice she began to tell Junie where to find a room.

It wasn't bad. The bed was clean. There was a Bible in the bottom dresser drawer. In the front of the Bible someone had written *God is good*, and underneath that, *God forgives all*. Junie wanted to write *Even me*, but she couldn't find a pencil.

She put Petey to bed in a clean diaper, leaving on his little shirt and his socks. During the night there was laughter and other noises in the hall, and once somebody fell against the door so hard that the panel made a cracking noise. Junie felt comforted by the sounds, the nearness of other people. She wasn't really alone, she thought.

She didn't feel alone until she went out the next morning and heard the news broadcast in the coffee shop where she had breakfast.

At first she didn't realize that the broadcast was about her and Petey. Somebody had kidnaped Peter Bentley Arnold, aged eleven months. The public was asked to be on the watch for June Campbell, aged 22, five foot four, weight 150 pounds, wearing a ...

June Campbell.

That's me, she thought, almost getting to her feet. She was in a booth, a very small booth back near the kitchen, with Petey squeezed in against the wall. They were eating oatmeal. The little cafe was warm and steamy and pleasantly filled with the odor of fried bacon. The radio speaker was almost directly over Junie's head.

She looked around to see if anyone was watching her.

The waitress noticed and came right over. "More coffee?"

"Thank you." Junie waited, expecting the woman to notice Petey now and to ask, isn't this the baby who was kidnaped, and Junie was going to say, yes, they were going to put him down the sewer, so I had to run away. But the waitress merely went back for the coffee pot and returned to fill up Junie's cup.

It occurred to Junie that she had better leave the city. She must get away from the radio broadcasts.

Everyone would be listening, even the Arnolds—they'd hear about it now—and then for the first time Junie realized that the Arnolds must be the ones who had started the broadcasts in the first place. Of course.

... if you see this woman with this child, please notify the police at this emergency number—

Junie fed Petey a spoonful of oatmeal and kissed the hand that he put against her mouth.

We repeat—this is urgent—please notify the police ...

Junie formed the words to herself: the police. Notify the police.

She suddenly felt cold, empty, and scared. Not scared the way she'd been yesterday, at the Arnolds'. Then, she'd been afraid for Petey, for what might happen to him, and running away with him had been a great relief, almost *fun*, with the feeling that she was finally going to fix things. Now she had to, run again, but it wouldn't be any fun at all. Junie didn't understand why this was so, even as she sensed its truth.

Urged by a sudden apprehension, Junie took out her small purse and counted her money. There was very little left. She hadn't realized how much it would cost to eat and to sleep, and to ride buses.

When she had paid for the breakfast there was hardly any money left at all. More scared than ever, she carried Petey out into the street. There were no radio broadcasts out here on the sidewalk but Junie felt conspicuous and exposed. Passersby glanced at Petey in her arms, and surely pretty soon one of them would run off to notify the police.

There was a friendly-looking man who had a newsstand. He wore an old sweater, pulled up around his ears, and a knitted cap. His face was red. When Junie paused there, trying to think, he made clucking sounds at Petey, and called him Old Top.

Junie turned to him as she had to the woman on the bus. "I want to get out of town the cheapest way I can," she told him.

"Lady," he said, "the cheapest way to get out of this town is on the Staten Island Ferry. You can go for a nickel and Old Top here can go for nothing."

"Oh, thank you. And how do I get to it?"

"Bus over there. See where the curb's painted yellow? Get the one says South Ferry."

"Would you write it out, please?"

Without curiosity he did laborious lettering on a scrap of newspaper, wetting the pencil stub in his mouth.

Junie wanted to ask, what is a ferry, but explaining it might take time. And something was telling her now that she had better hurry.

At the end of the bus line there weren't a lot of people getting off, but there were enough so that Junie could follow along and find her way and do the right thing without having to ask. The ferry ride was so nice that for a while Junie forgot about being scared, and running, and what might happen to Petey if they gave him back to his father and mother. She took in all the strangeness of being on the water, the sights and sounds of the harbor, the movement of the ferryboat under her feet, the smells of the sea.

She recognized the Statue of Liberty from a picture in a textbook she had seen at Sylvan Slopes, a feeling of stunned happiness coming over her; she hadn't really connected the picture with anything that actually existed, until now.

She thought, if I had time to take a hundred bus trips, I'll bet I'd see other things out of that book. Maybe they're all real and maybe they're all right around here someplace. And then, standing on the deck of the ferryboat in the sunshine, it seemed to Junie that she understood all at once that the world was a beautiful place, that the sky was benign—a sheltering blue umbrella under which everyone could live at peace.

I love everybody in the world, she thought.

Petey most of all, of course.

Not sure what she would find at the end of the ferry ride, Junie bought three egg-salad sandwiches at the lunch counter below, wrapped them in a paper napkin, and put them in her coat pocket. The ferry came into its slip, bumping and sloshing—a scary time—and then Junie saw that the people were hurrying ashore.

She saw the policeman, too.

He was tall, and he looked enormous and frightening in his blue uniform. He was carefully looking at everyone who came off the ferryboat. Junie's first instinct was to duck back out of sight, to hide on the boat somewhere.

She actually turned to run, but then she saw that a man who worked on the boat—he was doing something with a big rope—was watching her. His eyes were dark and moved quickly; they ran all over Junie as if they were memorizing her appearance.

She was choking with fear now, and her arms were so leaden it seemed that Petey was going to fall out of them and tumble to the deck.

Suddenly the man finished what he was doing with the rope and came over quickly—Junie was rooted to the deck—and he said, "Can I help you with the baby, ma'am? He's kind of heavy, isn't he?" And he took Petey easily in his big hands and Petey clung to the front of the man's leather jacket.

They walked up the ramp that connected the boat with the dock and went right past the policeman, who gave them an interested glance, as if he'd been told to look over *all* babies—only of course this wasn't the right one. Then by some miracle they were in another big room, almost a duplicate of the one Junie had waited in on the other side of the water.

The man tickled Petey under the chin, then gave him back to Junie. "He's sure a nice big husky kid," the man said.

"Thank you so much."

"It's not far to your bus now."

"Thank you so much," Junie repeated.

The man gave off a sea smell of tar and salt, and the sound of his voice was quiet and kind; the way he handled Petey showed how strong he was, and yet how gentle. Junie thought, I'll never see this man again, and there was a sudden ache around her heart, and a quick stinging of tears in her eyes as he turned away.

She had always wondered how you met a man, how you got acquainted with a man—the way Mrs. Arnold must have gotten acquainted with Mr. Arnold; and now she thought, it must be *this* way. Only for me it doesn't count, because I can't stop, I have to look after Petey.

At the end of the bus line she began to walk. She didn't stop until she found a nice beach. She put Petey down on his blanket and sat beside him. Petey seemed tired now; he looked at the ocean, at the waves rolling in, but he didn't try to find things in the sand and he didn't even want to taste his fingers. After a while he slid over to lie down, and went to sleep.

A woman and three boys of various sizes came to the beach. The boys ran and hollered, and the woman read a book. Junie would have liked to talk to the woman, but the woman wore an air of indifference, of defending herself by this indifference, as if the boys had worn away any ability she had to put up with other people. By and by the biggest boy yelled, "Mom, we're going around to the other beach and look at the old boat."

"Go ahead," the mother yelled back, not looking up from her book.

When the woman and the boys left, Junie went to see what was to be seen on the other beach. She rounded a crumbling small headland and came to a crescent of sand with an old rowboat lying on it. This beach was much more sheltered than theirs, so she picked up the sleeping baby and took him to it.

She investigated the boat. There didn't seem much wrong with it, except that it lay tipped on its side and there was a lot of sand in it, mixed with some orange peels and seaweed. Junie experimented out of curiosity, trying to straighten the boat. She was surprised at how heavy it was, and was unable to move it.

When Petey woke up she fed him one of the sandwiches. She built a sand castle for him, and let Petey knock it down. She took some seaweed out of his mouth.

At first there was just one siren, howling and whining far away, and Junie didn't pay any attention to it. In the city she had seen police cars on the avenue, and fire trucks, and she knew that the howling and whining came from one of these.

After a while, though, there were more sirens. They made Junie think of some sort of queer bird flying back and forth, emitting strange cries, hunting for something.

Hunting for something.

Junie scooped up the baby and the package of diapers, rushed to the rowboat, and crouched there, hiding.

It made a fine place to hide. The bow of the boat was turned a little so that the inside of the boat could not be seen from the bluff behind the beach. Junie listened to the sirens, now close, now far, and Petey chewed on one of the sandy orange peels. Though the air high above seemed to throb, to be filled with the noise of the sirens, right here there was a little island of stillness. She and Petey were shut away from the wind, from the sight of other eyes, from the howls given out by the strange hunting birds—from everything but the sun.

And the sun would not tell anyone where they were ...

The sea turned gray, cold-looking. A fog began to gather, at first offshore like a misty wall hanging out of the sky, and then creeping slowly shoreward, so slowly that you couldn't see it coming. You smelled it first in the air—a wetness with a flavor of fish and salt.

Junie made a bed for the baby with her coat, snuggling him down so that the dampness and chill would not make his sniffles worse. She kissed each of his eyes to make them close, the way she had always done at the apartment, and Petey's fingers strayed out to tangle in her hair.

"Nice Petey!"

Lying beside him, she kissed the end of his nose.

"My Petey. My own, own, own Petey!" She spoke out loud, dreamily. No one could hear. No one could say, Stop it. And Miss Gombie and the Arnolds were far away.

After a while there were voices, echoing queerly in the fog from the top of the bluff. One man kept calling, "Hey, Joe. Over here," and after a while another man yelled, "Hell, there's nobody. It's a bum steer, that's all."

Junie slept, and when she woke she was shivering. The night had come and the only paleness in all the dark was Petey's sleeping face. She tried to cuddle under the edge of the coat, to share a little of its warmth, and then suddenly she realized that when she had moved, the boat moved.

She experimented, puzzled, but it was true. When her weight shifted the boat rocked on its bottom.

"Rock, rock, old boat," she said aloud, wanting to laugh at the queerness, and then she stuck a hand over the side into the dark, and found cold water there. She sat up.

The fog must be thick, thick, thick—its wetness pressed against her face and filled her lungs. She stared, but her eyes found no prick of light in the night; it was like looking into a tunnel, or into a well, or like being shut in Miss Gombie's coat closet when you were bad.

"They can't find us now, Petey. We can stay all night in our boat. We'll sail away, even. Tomorrow we'll wake up and we'll be somewhere else."

She kissed Petey's forehead and rubbed his cheek with her cheek. Then she rocked and rocked the boat, but though it moved in a kind of trough, it never did sail away. Junie thought, I'll have to push it.

The voices were back at the top of the bluff now; a man was yelling about bringing the light. "Bring the damned thing over *here!*" And then there was a great moonlike glow, all gold and strongly shining. Junie, in the water beside the boat, was wet to her knees. The coldness, the force of the current, were startling.

A sudden sucking current pulled the boat away, off into the dark, and for a heart-stopping moment Junie thought that it had gone, taking Petey and leaving her stranded on the beach. But then, by a dim reflection from the big light beginning to swing back and forth at the top of the bluff, she saw the stern, dipping against the surf. She caught the rim of the boat and jumped in.

The current took them off quickly. Junie could tell how quickly by the way the big light on the bluff diminished through the fog. She sang softly to Petey and the surf slapped the hull and every once in a while the boat made a quick turnabout, end around end, that almost left her dizzy.

"We're sailing away, away. I'm all wet but I'll be dry," she sang. "By and by, Petey, by and by."

She had gotten dreadfully wet from the ocean—so wet that it took a while for her to understand that all the water was not coming off her clothes. Some of it was bubbling up through tiny broken places in the bottom of the boat.

She tried stuffing the edges of Petey's blanket into the broken places, and finally parts of her coat; but when she realized that these were not going to keep out the sea, she picked up the still-sleeping baby and stood, balancing herself against the boat's movement, holding Petey as high as she could, waiting, loving everybody, and remembering the sky as she had seen it from the deck of the ferryboat that morning.

The End

Blueprint for Murder

by Dolores Hitchens

"The way to kill an old person," said Mr. Harvod, "is just to let them die." He had the wineglass poised at his lips; behind it he grinned archly.

Young Tenny grinned back across the expanse of white linen and slender tapers of crystal and silver. "But suppose the old person decides not to oblige, like. Suppose he or she doesn't turn up toes just because you wish it? So then what?"

His uncle set down the wineglass. The wine shone like a jewel, full of shimmering reflections. "There's more to it than that, of course. But old age is fragile."

As if to add emphasis to this point, his uncle's voice hoarsened and trembled. And the hand at the base of the wineglass quivered as it withdrew.

"When you take away all reason for wanting to live," Mr. Harvod continued, "an old person is inclined to fade. Just to fade away. I observed this among my relatives at a fairly early age."

Again he smiled at Tenny, and offered the wine bottle, at which Tenny shook his head and murmured, "Thank you."

"I killed my Aunt Susan that way," his uncle said almost casually. "Just deprived her. Got the right kind of nurse to neglect her. Her bed always smelly and disordered, her hair matted and nails left untrimmed. No shoes if she should happen to want to get out of bed. No robe, either."

Tenny shook his head, but whether in dismay or in admiration it would have been hard for anyone to tell.

Mr. Harvod sat up straighter in the wheel chair and his face took on the expression of a memory well savored. "She had a little dog she was fond of. It disappeared. And her pet bird died. It lay in its cage for several days before anyone got round to taking it away. The rosebush outside her window, a climber full of yellow blooms, got broken somehow."

Tenny seemed suddenly subdued. He drank half of his wine and took several bites off his plate. "You felt good about all this?"

Mr. Harvod shrugged inside the satin robe with its splendid lapels. The two men were high above the city and the last of the daylight was dying beyond the silk-shrouded windows. The apartment seemed suddenly stilled, expectant, as if waiting to know how the old man had felt about committing murder.

"I was doing her a favor," Mr. Harvod said. "She was old and incurably sick and part of the sickness was this fierce desire to cling to life, to think of life as worth possessing. I simply arranged things so that living didn't look that rosy, and soon she became willing to let go."

"How did she do that?"

"Turned her face to the wall one day. Three days later she was gone. We cleaned up before we called the doctor and the undertaker. The nurse and I."

"The nurse was in on it?" Tenny was now making hefty inroads on the lobster.

"Not really, if you understand. She was just a slovenly woman doing what came naturally. I paid her a small bonus and it surprised her very much. She knew what she was. She didn't comprehend what I was."

"A villain without a flaw," Tenny responded admiringly, and his uncle giggled. "You never felt a moment's remorse or softening?"

His uncle's face sobered as if Tenny had said something unpardonable, but he replied at once. "Well, of course, Tenny, I had wee moments of weakness. Wouldn't anyone? The worst one, I'll admit, was when I took the dead bird away, and then for an instant my eyes met those of my aunt, with her lying there on those rumpled and stained pillows and me in my new clothes. I was already spending the money, you see. In that little time that

we looked at each other, *directly* at each other, I could see this—
well, this beseeching kind of thing. In her eyes."

The old man made an impatient, dismissing gesture with the
hand holding the fork and narrowly missed overturning his
wineglass.

Marshall the manservant stuck his white-haired head in from
the kitchen to see how they were doing, and discreetly withdrew.
Tenny noted the brief intrusion. Marshall, he thought—yes,
Marshall would have to go. Retired, replaced by someone more
suitable. There would be a third one, he decided. Marshall's
replacement wouldn't prove out and then there would be another,
the final choice. The nonpareil. He grinned crookedly to himself.
"You got over those moments of weakness?"

"Oh, yes. They were only passing moments. I had the main thing
in mind all the time. I never looked directly at Aunt Susan
again."

Tenny picked up his glass. "I do love this wine. May I have
another bottle or two? After all, it was you who spoiled me."

"Well, certainly. What I have is yours, Tenny."

So true. But in the back of Tenny's mind was a worry. How many
times had his uncle told that story of Aunt Susan and how many
people might have heard him? There was no statute of limitations
on murder, and might be none on inheritances gained thereby. He
really had to be shut up.

When dinner was over, Tenny strolled the length of the room
and gazed down through a window at the darkness of Central
Park below, and at the banks of lights beyond. No hum of traffic,
no sound of horn or siren penetrated to this anachronism of an
apartment high in its niche. It was old and well built.

While he was near the window Tenny brushed the potted plants
in their rack and thrust a nail through the main stem of that new
plant his uncle had been puttering over when Tenny had arrived.
Tenny's fingers skillfully drew up the potting mix to cover the
wound before he moved on.

When at last he said goodbye and had let Marshall help him
into his coat, he went down in the elevator and wasted no time

going to the desk to speak to the lobbyman. "My uncle wants me to take some more of his wine. I left a bag here when I came in."

The lobbyman was near-sighted and somewhat deaf; it took a little time to straighten him out and retrieve the outsized shopping bag. In the cellar he chose half a dozen choice bottles. He had an excellent market for them.

Remembering his uncle's words, he smiled dryly: he was already spending the money.

Nice to have a blueprint, he added, his smile brightening—a blueprint supplied by the victim, no less. Nice, really nice.

As Tenny stood at the curb, the bag of wine at his feet, waiting for a cab, he had an instant's temptation to turn and look up. To search for the wispy face which would be peering down at him from that high window. His shoulders tensed to lift his head backward, but then he put the idea firmly behind him. He might, staring up in the near-dark, imagine a touch of—what was the word his uncle had used? Beseeching. That was it. He might imagine a touch of that and it was best not to have it to remember later.

In the cab he set the bag of wine carefully beside him. If his uncle had seen it and later commented on its size, he could say he'd left a bundle with the lobbyman—things he'd shopped for earlier. Not that his uncle would remember to say anything. Most of the time now the old man's mind seemed quite confused. Only on the subject of Aunt Susan was he completely clear.

Tenny let his thoughts fly ahead to his own apartment, small but snug, full of his own choices in music and books and prints, and where Inez might be waiting for him.

One thing to keep in mind, he recalled.

I will never, he told himself, look the old man directly in the eyes again. This decision made, Tenny relaxed against the cushion of the cab seat.

The End

DOLORES HITCHENS BIBLIOGRAPHY
(1907-1973)

Novels:

As by Dolores Hitchens

Jim Sader mysteries
Sleep with Strangers (1955)
Sleep with Slander (1960)

Standalone books:
Stairway to an Empty Room (1951)
Nets to Catch the Wind (1952; reprinted as *Widows Won't Wait*, 1954)
Terror Lurks in Darkness (1953)
Beat Back the Tide (1954; abridged as *The Fatal Flirt*, 1954)
Fool's Gold (1958)
The Watcher (1959)
Footsteps in the Night (1961)
The Abductor (1962)
The Bank with the Bamboo Door (1965)
The Man Who Cried All the Way Home (1966)
Postscript to Nightmare (1967; UK as *Cabin of Fear*, 1968)
A Collection of Strangers (1969; UK as *Collection of Strangers*, 1970)
The Baxter Letters (1971)
In a House Unknown (1973)

As by Bert and Dolores Hitchens

F.O.B. Murder (1955)
One-Way Ticket (1956)
End of the Line (1957)

The Man Who Followed Women (1959)
The Grudge (1963)

Short Stories/Magazine Novels:

Stairway to an Empty Room (*Collier's*, Mar 31, Apr 7, Apr 14, Apr 21, Apr 28 1951)
Strip for Murder (*Mercury Mystery Magazine*, Oct 1958)
The Watcher (*Cosmopolitan*, May 1959)
Footsteps in the Dark (*Cosmopolitan*, Feb 1961)
Abductor! Abductor! Abductor! (*Cosmopolitan*, July 1961)
The Unloved (*Redbook,* Oct 1965)
If You See This Woman (*Ellery Queen's Mystery Magazine,* Jan 1966)
Postscript to Nightmare (*Cosmopolitan*, June 1967)
A Collection of Strangers (*Redbook*, Sept 1969)
The Baxter Letters (*Star Weekly*, June 26 1971)
Blueprint for Murder (*Ellery Queen's Mystery Magazine*, Aug 1973)

As by D. B. Olsen

Rachel Murdock mysteries
Cat Saw Murder (1939)
Alarm of Black Cat (1942)
Catspaw for Murder (1943; reprinted as *Cat's Claw*, 1943)

The Cat Wears a Noose (1944)
Cats Don't Smile (1945)
Cats Don't Need Coffins (1946)
Cats Have Tall Shadows (1948)
The Cat Wears a Mask (1949)
Death Wears Cat's Eyes (1950)
Cat and Capricorn (1951)
The Cat Walk (1953)
Death Walks on Cat Feet (1956)

Prof. A. Pennyfeather mysteries
Shroud for the Bride (1945;
   reprinted as *Bring the Bride a
   Shroud*, 1945)
Gallows for the Groom (1947)
Devious Design (1948)
Something About Midnight
   (1950)
Love Me in Death (1951)
Enrollment Cancelled (1952;
   reprinted as *Dead Babes in the
   Wood*, 1954)

Lt. Stephen Mayhew mysteries
The Clue in the Clay (1938)
Death Cuts a Silhouette (1939)

Stories by D. B. Olsen

Miss Rachel on Vacation [Rachel
   Murdock] (*Detective Story
   Magazine*, Sept 1947)
Murder Walks a Strange Path
   [Rachel Murdock] (*Detective
   Story Magazine*, March 1948;
   reprinted as "The Fuzzy
   Things", *Four-&-Twenty
   Bloodhounds*, 1950)
The Snake Dance (*Detective
   Story Magazine*, May 1948)
Alibi in Ice (*Detective Story
   Magazine*, Spring 1949)
As by Dolan Birkley

Blue Geranium (1944)
The Unloved (1965)

As by Noel Burke

Shivering Bough (1942)

Plays:

A Cookie for Henry: one-act play
   for six women (1941, as Dolores
   Birk Hitchens)

Tension-filled suspense classics from...

Dolores Hitchens

**Stairway to an Empty Room /
Terror Lurks in Darkness
978-1-944520-79-3 $19.95**
Two terrific crime novels from the
author of *Sleep With Strangers.*
"High-grade suspense."
—*San Francisco Chronicle.*
"Expertly tautened action and style."
—*Saturday Review.*

**Footsteps in the Night /
Beat Back the Tide
978-1-944520-93-9 $19.95**
"Horrible possibilities unfold and the
pace picks up, leaving us breathless
and horrified as we desperately flick
the pages to discover just how bad it's
going to get."
—Val McDermid, *New York Times.*

**The Abductor /
The Bank With the Bamboo Door
978-1-951473-27-3 $19.95**
"The suspense builds and
builds....Dolores Hitchens at her
best."—*Springfield Leader and Press.*
"Tense and exciting"—Francis Iles, *The
Guardian.*

**Bert & Dolores Hitchens
End of the Line
978-1-944520-57-1 $9.99**
"Bert and Dolores Hitchens' railroad
mysteries are among the very best of
their kind."—Bill Pronzini.
"Recommended."—*Mystery*File.*
Black Gat #17.

"Hitchens' work is incredibly varied but consistent when it
comes to depth of character and plotting."—Paul Burke, *NB*

"...there are so many secrets held by nearly all of the
characters that our curiosity increases along with the suspense
as each of the novels progresses."—Alan Cranis, *Bookgasm*

Stark House Press
1315 H Street, Eureka, CA 95501
707-498-3135 · griffinskye3@sbcglobal.net
www.starkhousepress.com
Available from the publisher, Ingram Books or Baker & Taylor Books.

**STARK
HOUSE**